KU-672-852

SIGHT

SIGHT

A. M. VRETTOS

EGMONT

EGMONT

We bring stories to life

This edition published 2007
by Egmont UK Limited
239 Kensington High Street
London W8 6SA

Text copyright © 2007 Adrienne Maria Vrettos
Cover copyright © 2007 Getty Images and Alice Barker

The moral rights of the author and cover illustrator have been asserted

ISBN 978 1 4052 3278 4

1 3 5 7 9 10 8 6 4 2

www.egmont.co.uk
www.adriennemariavrettos.com

A CIP catalogue record for this title is available from the British Library

Typeset in Goudy by Avon DataSet Ltd, Bidford on Avon, Warwickshire
Printed and bound in Great Britain by the CPI Group

Praise for Skin by A.M. Vrettos

'An absorbing account and one to be recommended.'
Bookseller

'An unusually intelligent and perceptive book written in
a confident and engaging style.' *Books for Keeps*

'A marvellous debut featuring an unforgettable
character.' *Kirkus Reviews, U.S.A*

'Vrettos is a writer to watch.' *Publishing News*

'A powerful and moving story . . . An honest and
unflinching portrayal of the effects of anorexia.
An excellent first novel.'
Annie Everall, Bookseller Children's Buyer's Guide

'Vrettos steers clear of melodrama and, instead, portrays
unexpected ways of grieving that, in turn, seem all the
more real in their specificity. In this bold first novel,
Vrettos captures the emotional complexities of a family
caught up in a disease beyond anyone's control.'
Horn Book Magazine, U.S.A

Drifter, Drifter's gonna gettcha

His head's on fire
And his eyes are black
First snow's coming and he's coming back

You can't hide under the bed
He'll find you and crack your head

You'll see his face in someone else
And she won't know, even herself

He got Clarence and he'll get you too
Drifter, Drifter's coming for you

1

It is a wide-sky darkness, made pale by a full moon rising and the desert sand reflecting its glow. We follow a dirt road, our headlights devouring the tracks we made just hours ago, when there was still daylight, and hope. In every direction the desert and the night sky are following in each other's footsteps, pushing further and further into the empty distance until their edges press together at the horizon.

In my troubled half sleep the rocking of the truck makes me dream that we are a bird and the desert plains are our wings. We are soaring, and we are falling. I jerk myself awake before we hit the ground. Deputy Pesquera, in the driver's seat, glances over at me. Her uniform presses, limp and wrinkled, against her large frame; the carefully ironed creases of the uniform sweated loose in the cramped and airless interview room back in Salvation.

'It takes a lot out of you, doesn't it, Dylan?' she asks, straightening her back in a stretch that brushes the top of her head against the truck's roof. Her sheriff department hat lies in the backseat. Mom says Deputy Pesquera is big-boned. My friend Frank says she's the best-looking linebacker he's ever seen.

I turn around in my seat and look through the back window, beyond the washed-out red of our tail lights and down the road disappearing into the darkness behind us. Far in the distance I see the bare-bulbed lights of the low and wind-worn cement buildings that make up Salvation's town centre.

We took the back route off Pine Mountain to get here, slowly winding our way down the little-used road, flanked by slopes of dry dirt and rock, instead of the thick groves of trees that cover the front side of the mountain. Rounding each blind corner, Deputy Pesquera would honk, warning anyone coming the other way to move back to their side of the narrow road. We stop about halfway down the mountain, in Baker's Creek – the tiny town that's built into the only grove of scraggly trees on the back side of the mountain.

There's no creek. The place is named for an old mountain guy named Baker, who fought with the county to have a water supply put in. I stay in the truck when the deputy goes into Sheboa's new grocery store. They used to have a store up on our side of the mountain, right in the centre of the village, but Mr Sheboa said he got tired of the new Village Business Association making up rules he didn't want to follow – rules that only made things better for the flatlanders that clogged up the mountain on weekends. I keep the hood of my black sweatshirt up while I wait in the truck, even though there is no hint of the late fall chill I'd felt while I waited for the bus this morning. I pull the strings on either side of the hood and cinch the face opening as small as it will go, until all sound is muffled and only the very edge of daylight can press against my closed eyes.

The thing about visions is, they hurt.

Darkness helps. It keeps the light from slicing behind the whites of my eyes and poking at the sore spot in my brain, the spot where, as I sit sweating outside Sheboa's grocery store, a flicking, pulsing picture shows itself to me again and again and again.

The good thing is, I was already sitting down when the vision first hit. There wasn't a long way to fall. In the vision I was in the desert, and it was dark. There was a hole dug in the sand in front of me, and a blue plastic barrel beside it. I was looking into the barrel. There was a girl inside, maybe ten years old. She looked up at me. There was black dirt caked at the corners of her mouth, and when she reached up for me, I saw her knuckles were bruised and torn. She'd fought.

When I came to, lying on the floor of the girls' bathroom, I saw three pairs of feet standing by the stall door. My friend Pilar, in black Converse high-tops like mine, peeked under the door first, holding her long braid to keep it from touching the floor. 'Dude,' she said, 'did you just fall off the can?' Thea, in the black studded stiletto-heeled boots was next, squatting down and scowling at me.

'You drop a tampon?' MayBe's handmade ankle-length flannel skirt mushroomed out around her when she kneeled down to get a look at me. 'You're OK, right? You might want to wash your face, though,' she said as I lifted my head, peeling my cheek away from the tile floor. I lied to them. I lied so well that they laughed when I re-enacted losing my balance while I reached for the toilet paper. Pilar still insisted on walking me to the nurse's office so I could get an aspirin, but I wouldn't let her wait for me there. I called the deputy from the nurse's office. 'I've been expecting your call,' she said.

*

The back side of the mountain slides right into the desert, the slopes of dirt and rock flattening out into an endless plain that makes my head ache when I peek out of my sweatshirt and try to see its end.

When we get to Salvation, Deputy Pesquera drives slowly through the town, looking to see which of the small cement buildings is the police station. I stare out the window at the rusted metal screen doors and the faded signs marking the post office, grocery store, and restaurant. The restaurant is called The Devil's Chow, and we wait there for the local sheriff, who is *Out in the flats*, according to the note taped to the door of the police station.

Like the other buildings in town, The Devil's Chow is long and narrow with no windows. The set-up of the restaurant gives anyone standing in the doorway a full view of everyone inside. And, I realise as we stand there, it gives anyone inside a good look at who is coming in. There are two rows of five small plastic tables running parallel to the bar, a glass soda-bottle vase filled with desert wildflowers on each table. The tables are empty, but four of the five wooden stools at the bar are filled by slumping men in cowboy hats, who glance at us long enough to look us down, up, and down again, their faces

7

shadowed by the brims of their hats. One of them smirks at the badge on the deputy's chest and then looks back up with the others at the TV mounted in the corner.

'Can't we just wait in the truck?' I whisper.

'Sit wherever you'd like,' the lady behind the bar says, not turning to look at us from where she is wiping down square bottles half-filled with liquids of various browns. I watch her, and notice that she wipes the same bottles down over and over again.

I follow the deputy to the table closest to the door and sit down across from her. The men at the bar glance at us again. The lady behind the bar doesn't interrupt her cleaning to bring us menus or water, so I watch her wipe down bottle after bottle. I don't realise how closely I am watching her until she turns around and catches me looking.

'I forgot you were there!' she says, slapping her forehead so hard it makes me flinch. She grabs a water pitcher and two plastic glasses and walks over to our table. She clacks the glasses down in front of us, pulls two laminated menus out of her apron pocket and slaps them down on the table. There is a name tag hooked crookedly on the apron, reading *Sarah*.

'You the ones here for Sheriff Len?' Sarah asks the

deputy. 'You his friend from up Pine Mountain?'

She overfills our water glasses with a shaky hand, spilling water on to the table. She doesn't clean it up. I catch the drip with the sleeve of my sweatshirt before it can spill into my lap.

'Yep,' the deputy says.

'I went up there once, to Pine Mountain. Swam in the lake. Pretty place. Now, what was it I just heard about you all up there?' Sarah drums her fingers against the water pitcher and looks absently out the door. 'Something about . . .' She nods slightly with a faint grin. 'Paradise, right? You all voted and changed the name of the mountain from Pine to Paradise.'

The deputy smiles and nods her head. I wait for her to say what had really happened, but she doesn't. She just picks up the plastic menu.

'That was a flatlander vote,' I say, blinking against the pulsing fluorescent lights. Sarah looks at me. 'They only let the businesses vote, and most of them are owned by flatlander suck-ups. They're the ones who wanted to change the name. Not us. It's not really changed till 1st January.'

'So basically you locals got screwed?' Sarah says.

'Basically,' I answer.

'Well, shit,' she says, shaking her head. 'That sucks.'

For a long moment it seems like she is lost in thought about the injustice of our mountain being renamed out from under us. But then she looks down at me like she'd just noticed I was there. 'How about a cheeseburger?'

'Sure,' I say. The deputy nods too. 'Cokes and fries, too, please.'

'I'm going to make one up for Sheriff Len, too. He's out in the flats, looking for my daughter, Tessa.'

I swallow a gasp and look at Deputy Pesquera. She ignores me and says, 'Is that so?' to Sarah.

'My mom was watching Tess yesterday afternoon.'

Sarah keeps talking, but I can't look away from Deputy Pesquera. It feels like my insides have all gone brittle, and if I look away from the deputy, if I look at Sarah, my whole body would splinter apart in shame. It was her daughter, Tess, I'd seen in my vision this morning. And I knew that it was only a matter of hours before I broke Sarah's heart.

'I think I might be on . . . what do you call it? Autopilot? I'm going to pour you two your Cokes, tell Billy to make your burgers and fries, but really what I want to do', she says looking down at me like she couldn't believe it, 'is scream. Am I screaming?'

I shake my head.

'What are you all doing down here, anyway?' she asks, staring out the door again. 'Len said it was some kind of book report you were doing. You should wait though, to interview him, until he finds my . . .'

A truck with a decal reading *Salvation Sheriff's Department* passes by the restaurant. The tall man in the driver's seat doesn't turn to look at us. He keeps his head tilted down, the sheriff's hat shading his face. There is no one, no Tessa, in the seat next to him.

'You want, I can bring your order over to you,' Sarah says, still staring at the now-empty dirt road. 'I'll bring it over when it's ready. Len said I should stay here, but I can bring it over.'

'We'll just wait and take that to go, if you don't mind. It'll give the sheriff a few minutes to get settled,' Deputy Pesquera says.

'Suit yourself,' Sarah says, already walking away.

I lean my head back against the seat and close my eyes, faking a sleep that soon enough becomes real.

In the dream I'm standing in the wide, dark desert again, looking down into the hole that is deeper than it is wide. The large blue plastic barrel sits upright next to it, the adhesive from a peeled-off white label shining white in the moon's glow. Far in the distance I can see the murky outlines of downtown Salvation.

In the dream I think, *I'm not supposed to be here again.* I point to the barrel and say to the empty desert, *I told you. She's in there.* Behind me there is a sound of desert rocks knocking and crunching together. My whole body goes stiff. I stare at the town lights of Salvation in the distance. There is a sound of heavy footsteps coming closer. I am not alone out here.

In my sleep I think of the self-defence classes I took with my friends Pilar, MayBe, and Thea. *Poke the eyes. Punch the throat. Twist and pull the gunnysack. Do NOT be polite.* I scream when the arm slaps across my chest, and I wake up swaying hard to the right, the seat belt locking against me, my face smacking against the window and staying pressed there. I see my own eye's reflection in the window, and the sickening sight of the desert spinning around us. The crunch of the truck tyres locked and scraping on the dirt is deafening. The truck finally jerks to a stop, rocking a little until it settles.

We are skewed sideways, half-on and half-off the road, a cloud of dust and small rocks settling around us, loudly peppering the roof, windshield, and hood. Deputy

Pesquera is leaning forward and gripping the steering wheel with one arm. Her other arm is still pressed across me. *Mom-Arm*, Pilar and I call this, as in the arm your mom flings in front of you to keep you from flying out the windshield. Deputy Pesquera moves her arm away from me and places it on the steering wheel.

'What did you say?' she asks calmly, still staring straight ahead.

My brain is still stuck in that inky sludge between being awake and being asleep, and it takes me a moment to get my mouth to work. 'I was asleep.' I push against the door, slowly righting myself in my seat, and look at the reflection of my cheek in the window, the same one I hit the bathroom floor with this afternoon. It's already starting to bruise. 'Did we hit something?'

'We spun out,' the deputy says, and then she laughs. 'You must scare the crap out of your mom, yelling in your sleep like that. You sure scared the crap out of me.'

'I yelled?'

'Screamed like a pissed-off mountain lion is more like it. Sounded like you were about to eat someone's face off.'

'That's gross.'

'Well, you know,' she says, absently putting on the voice she uses at school assemblies. 'Those mountain lions are not cute little kitty cats. They will tear your face . . .'

'Is the truck OK?' I ask, looking through the windshield to where the headlights are pointed down a slope, casting a shadow against the brush below.

'Are *you* OK?' she asks, making me squint by turning on the overhead light. She looks hard into my face. 'You look all right. Probably get a bruise, though. How many fingers am I holding up?' she asks, holding up her middle finger.

I laugh, and push her hand away.

'I'll check the truck,' she says.

She leaves the door open, the electric *ding, ding, ding*, sounding lonely in the silence of the dark desert. Her boots crunch on the sand as she walks around the front of the truck into the light of the headlights, and then around to the back.

'Looks OK,' the deputy says, getting in and closing the door. 'You should sleep, Dylan,' she says as she backs the truck up and sets it right on the road before driving again.

'No, thanks.' I roll down my window, letting the cool wind wake up my skin.

'Bad dream?'

I shake my head. The thing about dreams is, I'm not supposed to have them.

'Do you mind some music?' she asks.

'Whatever keeps you awake,' I answer quickly, anxious for this conversation to end, for the chance to think the thoughts thrumming at the back of my mind.

'Oh, I'm awake, but this will keep me happy.' She switches on the radio and turns the knob until there's a break in the popping static. 'Thank God,' she says, hearing the guitar-heavy classic rock song humming through the speakers. 'I was afraid it'd be country.'

'How far to the mountain?' I ask.

'A few hours. We'll get in way before sunup, especially taking the front way up.'

I look out the window, letting my eyes lose their focus so that the dark desert streams by in a muddy blur.

My dreams stopped when my visions started. I was five years old, in kindergarten. This little kid in our class, Clarence, was kidnapped and killed on his way to school. At the very moment it happened, we were all sitting in a horseshoe shape on the cushy green story-time rug, singing 'Frosty the Snowman', our shoeless feet stretched out toward the heater so that our socks could dry. When we'd gotten to school, there had already been enough snow to make snow-angels on the playground, and as our socks dried, it looked like the snow had woven a thick white curtain outside the classroom windows.

The windows were steaming, making some of the paper snowflakes come loose and fall behind the bookshelves. Miss Donna, who was the teacher's helper and who we liked because she had a pretty voice and would sing us songs from the radio, walked around lightly squeezing our toes, to see if our socks were dry. Pilar and I kept lying on our backs and lifting up our feet to get her to squeeze them, so we could loudly whisper, 'Oh, no, I'm ticklish!' and then tuck our feet under our bums to hide them.

Then our teacher, Mrs Fenderson, motioned to Miss Donna like she was pretending to be on the telephone. Miss Donna nodded and stopped squeezing our toes. Something in my belly felt like it was slipping as I watched Miss Donna cross the room and pick up the phone on the wall by the door. The singing voices became a swollen, wordless hum underneath the sound of my own breathing and the terrible sound of the paper snowflakes unpeeling and falling from the windows. I watched Miss Donna's lips, and I saw her say the word 'Clarence'.

There was a feeling like when my dad would toss me up into the air and catch me again, a feeling like slipping on the wet dock and falling into the lake. My eyes rolled up, looking for darkness, my eyelids closed, and I saw Clarence. He was sleeping – but not sleeping – lying under a green tarp. I saw that he wasn't wearing his glasses or his favourite smooshy hat that was the same orangey-red colour as his hair. There was heavy snow weighing down the branches surrounding him. The tip of one branch bent so low that a cluster of pine needles, frozen into a point, touched his bare ankle where his dark blue jeans had ridden up. He had no boots on, and he had no socks.

I pulled my eyelids open with my fingers, making the white electric light of our classroom and the snow outside wash out the image and dilute it until it was gone. Then I threw up. It felt so *wrong*, what I'd seen. Like seeing your own guts, or eating someone else's boogers.

I didn't tell my mom what I'd seen, not for days, because I knew that seeing things was worse than anything. Worse than overflowing the sink in the bathroom or going to my neighbour Ben's without permission. Seeing things was so bad, I'd been afraid of it happening my whole life. Before Clarence, and sometimes even after, my mom would walk suddenly into my room when I was playing and ask me who I was talking to. My dolls, I would tell her, holding one up for her to see. Sometimes I would feel her watching me as I ate my lunch or worked on a puzzle or watched a cartoon. She would ask me in a shaky voice, 'Dylan, honey, are you seeing something?' I knew the right answer to that question, I knew to shake my head and say, 'No, Mommy.' Saying *no* to that question made my mom smile, made her hug me and tell me she loved me. I don't think I was lying to her. If I try to think back now, I don't *remember* seeing things, or talking to people that weren't there. But sometimes I think maybe I just wanted to disbelieve so much that I rubbed them out, erased them, like from a picture. Sometimes there are people-shaped holes in my memories.

Three days after Clarence disappeared, when they'd found his body in the woods, my mom and dad sat down on my bed to tell me softly that my friend had gone up to heaven. I'd been sick in bed since he'd disappeared, slipping in and out of a hot and restless sleep where the only dream that came was of Clarence, lying in the snow. After they told me, my dad got up to get my mom a tissue because she was crying. My mom smoothed my hair on my forehead, and the softness of her touch made the lump in my throat crack into a sob. She thought I was crying for Clarence, but I wasn't. I was crying for me. I was going to make my mom stop loving me because I wasn't strong enough to keep this secret any more. 'I'm sorry, Mommy,' I said.

Mom held me so tight when she carried me into the police station that the thick beads of her necklace bit into my collarbone. We had fibbed to Daddy and told him we were going to the doctor. Mom held me close until Sheriff Dean led us into his office, then she sat me on the edge of his desk and backed away from me, fingering the beads around her neck. Eleven years ago, Sheriff Dean was still the one you went to when something bad happened. He was the one who came when Thea's mom ran their Cadillac into a tree, and when someone stole the inflatable Santa Claus from in front of Sheboa's Grocery. Dean's still officially sheriff, but everybody knows he spends all his time in his office with his door closed, napping in his chair. It's Deputy Pesquera who does most of the real work now. But it was Sheriff Dean there when Clarence died, and it was him that Mom made me tell what I'd seen. I told him that Clarence's feet were cold from the snow, and that he'd lost his glasses. I said that he was near a big green plastic sheet that was hung between two trees, like when Mom let me make a fort in our den by spreading my Hello Kitty comforter between the chair and coffee table. I said that there was a man who was walking away from Clarence, leaning forward against the wind and the snow.

'She's right, isn't she?' my mom asked Sheriff Dean.

My mom didn't stop loving me. But I think now that maybe something in her love changed colour, shifted from all bright colours to some shadows and muddy greys. I know what that's like. It happened to me, when my dad left us. My love for him stayed, but it was coloured by the darkness of what he'd done.

Before that, though, when Daddy was still with us, when my mom brought me home from the police station that day, she said we shouldn't tell him what I'd seen. She said it was all gone now, and I didn't need to dream it any more. What I heard was: *You shouldn't dream, any more. Never again.* That's why my dreams come to me when I'm awake.

For months and months and years and years people were waiting for the Drifter to come back. To 'strike again', like the newscasters say. But he never came back. And he never showed up anywhere else, either. He never terrorised some other mountain town, or some other city, or some other anything. Sheriff Dean had the Drifter's DNA, and he would have it compared to other DNA found on other kids who had been killed, all over the country. We used to tell one another he kept the DNA in a safe, behind his refrigerator, because back then we didn't really know what DNA was. We thought it was a puzzle piece dropped out of the Drifter's body that he'd left behind, and all the police needed to do was find the body the piece fitted back into.

Back then I didn't think the Drifter had feet, because drifting seemed like something a ghost would do – float a foot above the ground, soundless and cold. I thought he floated off the mountain and into the sky. It made me feel better, to think that.

I think everybody eventually thought sort of the same thing, or at least fooled themselves into believing he'd gone one way or another. People don't really talk about him any more.

The texture under the tyres changes, the low rumble of the dirt road jolting into the smooth hum of pavement. Ahead of us the white neon lights of a gas station glow against the night sky. It's the first building we've seen in over a hundred miles, and I know from the drive out here that there won't be any others for about fifty miles more, until we get to the highway.

While the deputy pumps gas, I go inside the store and walk up and down the aisles, my stomach grumbling but my sleepy brain not able to make sense of the rows and rows of chips and canned ham. I end up at the orange counter that lines the window overlooking the gas pumps, watching the soft-bellied bean burrito I got in the freezer section turn slowly in the microwave's sick-looking yellow light. I can feel someone watching me, and when I can't see anyone to my left or right, I look up to see the counter man's reflection in the rounded security mirror mounted on the ceiling. He has his elbows resting on the counter, and he scowls at me when our eyes meet in the mirror. I look away, and see another reflection, this time of myself in the window. No wonder he scowled. I've got the hood of my black sweatshirt up, and my hands are shoved into its pockets, stretching the sweatshirt down so that my head is tipped back a little against its pull. I look at my tipped-up chin and the light bruise on my cheek in the reflection and think, *You talkin' to me?*

When Pilar and I drive cross-country, we'll be tough girls, glowering our way from truck stop to gas station to roadside diner. We'll smile only at waitresses, and we'll scowl at all the men. Maybe we'll kiss a boy or two before leaving them in the dust, but mostly we'll just strut with such long-legged attitude that everyone will assume we're on the run from the law.

You talkin' to me? I think again, imagining myself walking up to the man behind the counter.

'Ow!'

The deputy pulls my hair as she yanks down my hood.

'You're too cute to look like a convict,' she says. 'God, what is that smell? Are you going to eat that?' she asks, pointing to the rotating burrito.

I shrug, and run my fingers through my hair till it's sticking out in all directions. 'I'm hungry.'

The deputy looks at my hair and gives an exaggerated flinch. 'Suit yourself, tough guy.'

'That's "tough lady", thank you very much,' I say as the microwave beeps and the display blinks *Open, Open, Open.*

'Do you want water?' the deputy asks, walking away.

'Root beer,' I answer, trying to pull the burrito out of the microwave without burning myself. I end up wrapping it in paper towels.

The deputy has two large bottles of water and a package of trail mix sitting on the counter when I get there. I set the mummified burrito next to them, and head to the refrigerator to get my root beer.

When I get back to the counter, the deputy sighs. 'Well, I guess that will cover up the taste of that dead-dog burrito.'

When we're outside, the deputy says, 'He wanted to search your pockets.'

'What?'

She opens my door for me. 'He thought you were stealing.'

'I wasn't stealing,' I say to the slamming door. As soon as she gets in I say it again. 'I wasn't stealing.'

'You sure?' the deputy asks.

Even though I'm secretly thrilled the guy thought I was badass enough to pocket an extra burrito, I do a furious and very effective emptying of my empty pockets. The only thing that comes out is a school-picture-size photograph that slips through the air and lands next to the stick shift. The deputy picks up the photograph. Tessa had straight hair to her chin, her bangs cut high and crooked on her forehead. In the picture you can see she's missing her front teeth, and the teeth she does have are all pointing into each other. She looked like her mom.

'She was a cute kid,' the deputy says, handing it back to me. I slip it back into my pocket.

I wait till she's pulling out of the gas station driveway before I throw the burrito out the window, making sure I give the finger to the guy who's still watching us from behind the counter when I do.

24

The deputy slams on the brakes and makes me get out to pick up the burrito – which exploded into beany gooeyness when it hit the asphalt – and throw it in a trash can. She doesn't make me apologise to the guy, though, and she lets me pick the chocolate out of the trail mix, which I think is decent.

It's only an hour before the mountain is in front of us, jutting up out of the flatlands, the winding road to the top looking from a distance like a snake pulling the mountain back into the ground.

The further we get up the mountain, the greener the landscape gets, until the desert scrub and cactus have been replaced by thick groves of tall trees that tower over the road. We've kept the windows rolled down, even though the refreshing cool air of the desert has turned chilly and damp on the mountain. This road is officially called Highway 17, but everyone calls it either Up-Mountain Road or Down-Mountain Road, depending on which way you're heading. We follow it up to where it turns into Lakeshore Drive, the main road that circles our town, cutting right through the village.

Mom says people used to joke that the centre of town had anything you ever wanted, as long as all you wanted to do was drink a beer and shoot something. That was when it was still called the centre of town, before the Village Business Association voted to change the name to 'the village' because it made it seem more like a destination, more like 'an outdoor shopping plaza', which is how they describe it on the official Pine Mountain web site. Now that the gun store is gone and the liquor store's been remodelled to look like a place Santa Claus might live, the village is sort of painfully adorable. There are high wooden arches that curve over lakeshore at either end of the village, carved with the words *Welcome* on one side and *Thank you for visiting* on the other. For the quarter-mile stretch of road between the two arches, it's supposed to feel like you're in an alpine village, especially when it snows. I've never been to an alpine village, so I wouldn't know. From our village, though, I'd guess the alpine ones have cute little brown-shingled stores with white trim and hand-carved signs and tub-gutted flatlander husbands sitting on benches flanked by oversize wooden flowerpots, waiting for their flatlander wives to finish buying pine cone ornaments.

'Roll up your window,' the deputy's turned on the windshield wipers, smoothing away heavy drops of rain. 'Glad this didn't hit us on our way up-mountain. I bet it freezes before morning. First snow's coming soon.'

*

First snow's coming and he's coming back. We wrote that song about the Drifter together, Pilar, Thea, MayBe, and me. The summer after Clarence died, we spent a lot of time sitting in the shaded dirt under my back porch. Our house is built into the side of the mountain, so the back porch sits on stilts stretching twenty feet down. Even if we stood against the house, where the porch was closest to the ground, there was no way we could jump up high enough to touch the porch's underside.

We were allowed to sit under the porch when Mom was sitting in a lawn chair, reading under an umbrella, in the thin strip of grass between the back porch stilts and the chunk of forest that separates our house from our neighbours', the Abbotts'. Mom would glance up at us before she turned every page. Me and my friends sat in the dirt and made up that song, line by line, and then sang it quietly to ourselves over and over and over again.

It's weird, having happy memories of that song. Not the song so much, but what we'd do when we sang it. We'd sing the song almost absently, while we braided one another's hair, played cat's cradle, or dug holes in the dirt with twigs. The song was a soundtrack to that summer and, less and less, to the years after it. I felt safe, singing it, surrounded by my friends, my mom close by in her lawn chair. Even now, sometimes one of us will sing a snippet of the song in the same absent way.

Just past the village the constant curtain of trees that flank the road is interrupted by a wide and hard-packed dirt road that cuts straight down to the lake. I crane my neck to see the giant flattened patches of dirt that mark where the new houses are going to go up. A bulldozer with its scoop raised sits in the moonlight at the end of the row. Behind it the lake spreads out, houses dotting its shores.

At the top of the dirt road is a giant wooden sign, reading *The Willows: Own a Piece of the Forest in the Sky* and under that, scrawled in still-dripping red spray paint, is *You Prick*. Deputy Pesquera makes a growling sound in her throat. I look back out the window and see two figures crouched down at the foot of the sign, trying to hide from view behind one of the thick poles. Even in the shadows I recognise the square head and hulking figure of my friend Frank, and, next to him, the long-limbed gawkiness of Cray. I turn away from the window, trying to keep them from seeing me, and trying to keep the deputy's attention away from the sign. I glance at her, but she's still looking straight ahead. At first I think she didn't see anything, but then she says, 'You tell your friends they're playing with fire.'

I close my eyes.

'You're not asleep, Dylan,' she says. 'Tell them they're playing with fire and I'm the firehose that's going to put them out.'

I keep my eyes closed. 'I'm not going to tell them that.'

'Why not?' she asks sharply.

I sigh, and keep my eyelids pressed together. 'Because that's stupid. You're the firehose.'

'Fire . . . extinguisher?'

I shrug and then yawn so hard that I have to open my eyes. I look at her. 'I'll tell them they're playing with fire and you're going to piss them right out.'

She laughs hard, then points at me. 'Watch your mouth!' And then laughs again, slapping the steering wheel and breathing deep. 'Jeezum Crow, what a night. Right?'

'Yeah.'

'Are you all right?' she asks.

'I just need some sleep.'

'Tell your mom I'll call her tomorrow and brief her on what happened.'

I groan. 'You'll *brief* her?'

'You know the deal,' she says. 'It's either that or she comes with you next –' The deputy interrupts herself by clearing her throat.

I finish the sentence for her. 'Next time. And I don't want her to come with me. It's bad enough that you tell her what it's like.'

'I don't understand.' She sighs.

'No, you don't.' The thought of my mom there, watching me, makes my stomach clench. Embarrassment? No, shame.

The headlights do little to puncture the inky darkness of my dead-end street. This slope can feel almost vertical when you're driving up it on a snowy winter day. The only other house on the street is Ben Abbott's house. The Abbotts are downslope from us, so sometimes in the winter we end up just leaving our truck in their driveway and walking the rest of the way. As we pass by Ben's house, I see the rambling white farmhouse through the trees, and the barn beyond it.

'Ben's a good kid,' the deputy says.

I stifle a laugh. What does that even mean, *good kid*? I know what the deputy thinks it means. That she's never had to come down to the school to arrest him for slashing the tyres on a weekender's sports car, that she sees him at

Sheboa's or whatever the hell it's called now, with his mom and little brothers, carrying grocery bags for his mom. Ben *is* a good kid, even though he seems hell-bent on changing that. I'm surprised I didn't see him crouched down with Frank and Cray by the Willows sign. For a while now I've watched as he's gone through a sort of transformation. He's still the same Ben – with the crooked smile, flannel shirts, sort of smooshy face, and goofy laugh – but it's like he's trying to get himself a starring role on *When Good Kids Go Bad*, which even though it's not technically a TV show, it could be. It's sort of cringe-making to watch Ben laugh too loud at Frank's stupid blockhead jokes, and to watch the way Ben sort of postures that he's going to be this old mountain tough guy.

Deputy Pesquera pulls in behind Mom's truck. I'm so happy to see our little house with its A-shaped roof that I swallow back tears. I love how the roof slopes almost all the way to the ground to keep the snow from piling too high, and how its triangle shape looks just like the trees I used to draw when I was little.

'That's OK,' I say when the deputy starts to open her door. 'You said you'd brief her tomorrow, right?'

'Right. Well, good night, then.'

*

Inside the house I click the dead-bolt lock into place and wave at Deputy Pesquera through the window.

I drag myself up our narrow staircase and stand for a long time in front of the open bathroom door, scowling. There's a slow-motion debate going on in my head. Go pee now, and avoid getting up in the middle of the night and losing sleep. Skip the bathroom and go right to sleep, and get to sleep sooner. I decide to fall down where I am and sleep in the small hallway that connects my room, my mom's room, and the bathroom we share.

'Was it her?'

Mom's been watching my internal battle from her bedroom doorway. Instead of answering, I stand back up and go into the bathroom.

I sit on the toilet, and fall asleep. Mom wakes me up by knocking on the bathroom door and whispering, 'Was it her?'

I flush, to drown her out, and wash my hands. I don't brush my teeth and I don't wash my face, but I do put in my retainer. Mom has the unique and infuriating ability to tell if my teeth have shifted overnight.

I open the bathroom door and walk past Mom, giving her what I hope is a conversation-ending nod, and go into my room. I flop face-first on to my bed, the wrought iron bed frame creaking in protest. The covers jump and fall around me, and cover half of one leg. Good enough. I manage to flick off one shoe; the other hangs on to my big toe.

'Was it her?' Mom has ignored my nod.

I keep my eyes closed and groan, hoping she can tell it means yes.

'I'd hoped . . . it was a false alarm. Where was she?'

I don't answer. I want to sleep. I want to sink down, down, down into a warm dark empty place. She waits till I fall asleep for a moment and asks again, 'Where was she?'

My body stiffens. I don't lift my head, but say into my pillow, 'Can't you just watch the news like everybody else?'

She makes a clucking sound. She's not happy. She likes to know what I know, what I told the police, and what I saw. I sigh and roll over so I can glare at her. She sits on my bed and takes my hand. Then she starts to untangle my hair with her fingers.

'I want to sleep, Mom.'

'I know.'

She works my hair, and hums.

I'm still glaring at her. 'Then let me sleep.'

She shakes her head and whispers, 'Not yet. Where did they find her?'

I clench my jaw and sigh through my nose. Mom and I both highly value communication through sighing. She answers back with a whistler: making the slightest space between her lips and letting the air make a high-pitched exit. I keep my eyes locked with hers as my face reddens, my throat tightens, and tears burn my eyes.

'Where was she?' Mom whispers. She lies down, facing me, on the bed, and takes my hands in hers. I turn and bury my face in the pillow and cry.

She lets me. I finally turn to her, wiping my face on the pillow, and stammer out: 'In the desert outside of town. In a barrel that smelled . . . She thought it smelled like . . . Her dad had this chemical stuff he used to take the *My Child is an Honour Student* bumper sticker off of his truck . . .'

Mom shakes her head and makes an *Oh, no* noise. She rubs my back, which makes me cry harder.

'That's what it smelled like. It made her throw up and it felt like it was cutting into her head like when you stick your thumbnail in a lima bean and split it in half.'

Mom sighs and rolls over on to her back. She wipes her eyes with her robe. I watch more tears well up and roll down her cheeks.

'Mom, he knew. Her father knew. Right then, right

34

when she . . . He was thinking to her, *I'm with you, I'm with you, I'm with you.* She heard him, and then she died.'

I don't tell her about the dream, about the sound of crunching rocks behind me in the desert.

Mom cries for a little longer. Then she gusts out a cry-ending sigh and, standing up, says, 'You did good. Sleep now.'

She squeezes my hand and kisses me on the forehead.

She gets up and pulls the covers out from under me, so she can pull them over me. She lingers at the door and looks at me as she turns out the light.

'Good night,' she says.

'Night, Mom.'

I study the glowing stick-on star constellations on my ceiling. I'm emptied out. A slack balloon. It's what Mom wanted. She knows if I tell her about it, what I saw will leave me, at least for a while. Long enough for me to fall into a dreamless sleep. Mom will carry it into her room, sit in the chair by the window, and see it all for herself while I sleep.

2

Ever since my dad went on hiatus, Mom's been getting up before five o'clock every morning, no matter what's happened the night before. This means by the time she has to wake me for school at seven, she's had two cups of coffee and taken a run down to the lake and back again. So when she sticks her head into my room to wake me up this morning, she's too wired to gently rouse me from sleep with sweet cooing and a loving tug of my big toe. Instead I have my dreamless, perfect sleep split in half by Mom's full-volume voice saying, 'WELL, ARE YOU GOING TO SCHOOL OR AREN'T YOU?' There are no words for the rage this fills me with. It's actually what gets me out of bed, which I think is why she does it. I'm following her down the hall before my eyes are even fully open, before the memories of yesterday can pull down on my arms and hang like a weight from my neck.

'Mom!'

She glances at me over her shoulder and nods

approvingly. 'Going to school. Good choice.'

'*Mom!*'

'What?' She gives a wide-eyed smile that could make me spit hot lava. 'I whispered.'

'No, you didn't!'

'Are you sure you want to go to school today? You look tired,' she says.

'Of course I'm tired!' I yell. I yank out my retainer and throw it into the bathroom sink. 'I was down the hill all night!'

She inhales sharply and grabs my chin. 'Is that a bruise? Did somebody hit you?'

'Yeah, Mom, I totally got beat up by my psychic vision.'

'Dylan,' she says, and at first I think it's a low warning I hear in her voice. It's something else, though, something closer to pleading. She wants me to forget.

It takes me a second to find the energy to play along. I do, though, because I know if I make my body play along with *It's just another normal morning at the Driscoll house*, my heart will eventually believe it.

'And it's cold in here!' I say, stomping my foot. 'And it was *freezing* in my room last night,' I grouch, remembering waking up for a moment to a bedroom so cold I imagined I could see my breath in the moonlight.

'When can we start using the woodstove?'

'Tonight,' she says, smiling. 'If it stays this cold. Especially if it finally snows.'

She hugs me and I can hear her heart racing faster than her happy smile is letting on. She's playing along too.

'You're just so loud!' I say into her shoulder.

She laughs and squeezes me. 'I just wanted the day to start, darlin', and it wasn't going to start with you in bed.'

This is the closest she'll come to acknowledging what happened last night. Sure, she'll call the deputy today and get *briefed* and all that, but she won't mention it to me.

'Why can't you do this when you wake me up?' I say, wrapping my arms tighter around her waist. 'Why's there have to be so much yelling?'

'I didn't yell. And we're hugging now. *And* you're out of bed. Two birds, one stone. You need to get ready for school,' she says, pulling herself out of my arms and walking into the bathroom.

'So hugging me is like throwing a rock at a bird and killing it?' I ask, following her. I'm totally playing for time now, and she knows it.

She picks up her brush and runs it through her hair. 'Do you want to go to school today or not?' she asks, not looking at me.

'No!' If I weren't so tired, I'd stamp my foot when I say it.

She stops brushing. 'Because of last night, or because you're sixteen?'

'I'm sixteen-and-a-half,' I say.

She reaches behind me and turns on the shower. Sometimes I wish she'd sit on the edge of the tub and dump warm water over my soapy hair with a plastic pitcher, like she did when I was a kid. Instead she holds my face in her hands, gives a little gasp and a wide smile, and says, 'You're growing into your face!'

She's impossible to stay mad at. I look at myself in the mirror and can't help but smile.

But then she says, 'You look more and more like a Driscoll every day.'

I know she means to be sweet when she says this, like, *You're one of us*, but there's another *us* I want to be a part of too. My mom kept her last name when she married my dad, and when I was born, she insisted that I get her last name too. It took me a long time to realise that my dad's last name wasn't Driscoll, and even longer to realise that it must have really bothered him. When he corrected people on his name, he'd laugh without humour and say, 'No, no, I'm not a Driscoll. I'm just the donor.'

I remember a fight they had about it, right before he left. My mom said he could change his name to Driscoll if he wanted us all to have the same name so badly. 'That's what you want, isn't it?' she yelled, 'to be part of this family of freaks? Except you can't handle it. You can't handle what she can do . . .'

I wasn't supposed to be listening to them fight. I was supposed to be in my bedroom, playing 'pool party' with my dolls and the big iron pot we used to make popcorn, filled with water. I never asked my mom what she meant when she said *family of freaks*. I didn't want her to know I was listening.

'Go on in and get ready or you'll miss the bus,' my mom says, nudging me playfully into the bathroom. I close the door behind me and look at my face in the mirror. I can't help but smile.

When I was born, Mom's relatives looked at me through the Plexiglas window of the just-born baby unit, nodded at one another, and murmured their approval. I was a *really* ugly baby. I had the face of a full-grown woman planted on the body of a newborn. I was what Mom called a true Driscoll woman-to-be, with wide-set eyes, heavy lids, cleft chin, strong jaw, and high forehead. It was a face that would look fine on a grown-up, but on a baby, on a little kid, even, it looked completely ridiculous. It didn't help that I had, I kid you not, a baby-size mono-brow. I think even Mom, with all her 'Now stop it, you were a *beautiful* baby' talk, was glad when my face got big enough to separate the fuzz that grew straight and dark across my forehead. It wasn't till puberty that things began to even out, that my face stopped looking like it was too big for my body.

If you look through my baby book, there're no pictures of any of those ugly-loving relatives holding me. That's because as soon as the doctors let Mom go from the hospital, she and my dad wrapped me in the blanket from the baby ward, hopped on a cross-country bus, and took off. They ended up here, on Pine Mountain. I don't know what that trip was like for the other passengers on board the bus, but I know from Pilar's little sister, Grace, that newborn babies are pooping machines, and that when they're not pooping, they're crying. Mom says it wasn't that long of a trip, only a couple of days, but I'm guessing that it was a *long* couple of days for everyone involved.

It's not until the hot water has steamed up the mirror that I admit I'm having some sort of major malfunction involving getting my body into the shower. It's the sound of the water pelting the tile that's keeping me leaning against the sink, staring into the shower through the hot fog. The sound is like sand, whipped up by the wind and peppering against a blue plastic barrel.

I stick my fingers into my ears, close my eyes, and step into the shower.

I spend most of the shower sitting down, leaning over my legs, my fingers still in my ears, letting the hot water stream down my back, watching it swirl around my feet and down the drain.

Through my plugged ears I hear the muffled sound of Mom knocking on the door. She says that Dottie just drove by on the way up the hill.

Dottie's my bus driver, and my nemesis. She's been driving my bus to and from school since my very first day of kindergarten, which you would think would make her at least a little fond of me, but no. She lives to torment me. And the fact that she just drove by means that I have exactly six minutes before she gets to the dead end at the top of our street, turns around, and heads back down toward our driveway. And if I'm not standing there waiting, she'll drive on, leaving me in the dust. If she's feeling especially evil, she'll beep as she goes by.

I do a two-minute wash of the parts I imagine are particularly stinky, and hope Mom's pricey perfumed

42

lotion will take care of the rest. I try to save time by not using a towel and depending on the absorbing power of my clothing, but the combination of water and lotion has somehow turned into a glue that makes every bit of clothing I put on adhere to exactly the wrong body part. I run down the stairs, trying to yank down my sweatshirt from where it's wrapped like a scarf around my neck.

'Are those your same clothes from last night? You need socks!' Mom says, as I shove my bare feet into my high-tops. 'It's going to rain again today!'

The telephone rings and Mom and I both lunge for it on the end table. I get to it first.

'Hello?'

There's only silence on the other end.

'Hello?' I say again.

'Do you know who this is?' At first I think it's my aunt Peg, but even though there's the familiar slow lilt, there's a teasing tone that I know doesn't belong to my straight-laced aunt Peg. 'Who is this I'm talking to? Is that my niece, sounding all grown-up?'

'Yep, it's me, Auntie.'

'Who is it?' Mom asks loudly, reaching for the phone. 'Peg or Ruby?'

I swat at her hand and mouth the word 'Ruby'.

43

'Give me the phone,' Mom mouths back.

'Tell your mama,' my aunt says slowly, 'to let you talk to your auntie.'

I hold the phone to my chest. 'For your information, she wants to talk to me.'

'You'll be late for school,' Mom says, 'and you need socks.'

'How are you, Aunt Ruby?' I ask, while jumping up and dodging Mom's hand as she tries to grab the phone.

'Oh, I'm fine, darling, I'm just fine. How are you?'

I run upstairs to my room and open my sock drawer. Empty. 'I'm good,' I say. 'Just getting ready for school.'

'Oh, that sounds nice.'

I kneel down to look under my bed. No socks. I check under my bureau. Underwear, but no socks. Finally I jump up and grab a balled-up pair from the clothes hamper and head back downstairs.

'What are *you* doing, Auntie?' Even though we don't get to talk often, I know that Aunt Ruby always has the best answer to that question. Aunt Peg will just say, *Oh, I'm doing the laundry* or *Oh, just setting the dinner table*, but Aunt Ruby will always say something interesting.

'Oh, darling.' Aunt Ruby laughs, 'I'm just sitting here on the front porch filling that pickle jar.'

Most of the time I have no idea what she's talking about. Like now. Is she peeing in the pickle jar? Putting actual pickles in it? Catching spiders? I bet she catches spiders; she seems cool enough to do that. I sit back down on the couch with Mom.

'What do you mean, filling the pickle –'

Mom chooses this moment to have a silent hissy fit.

Aunt Ruby laughs quietly. 'Tell your mama not to worry herself. I'm not coming anywhere near her girl.'

Mom finally succeeds at unpeeling my fingers from the phone.

'Dylan has to catch the school bus, Ruby,' she says firmly into the phone. She points to the front door.

'Fine,' I grumble, pulling on my socks and shoving my feet into my high-tops. As I close the front door behind me, I hear Mom ask, 'How's Mama?' and then, 'Because I want to talk about Mama, not nonsense, that's why.'

Mom says she hasn't told either of her sisters about the things I see. I wish she would. It'd be easier, I think, if at least one of us told somebody.

Oh, crap. I see Dottie as soon as I close the front door. She's doing a slow roll by our driveway, but as soon as she sees me, she floors it. I launch myself off the porch, landing in a run that sends me tearing out of the driveway, chasing the bus down the street toward Ben's, the second stop on her route. It's midway through this run that Dottie and I share our special morning moment of Zen. I fall into a rhythm, running directly behind the bus, and every once in a while Dottie will glance at me in her rear-view mirror and I'll think, *That's right, you old crank, I'm still here.* And in her eyes I can see her thinking, *You will never catch me, you smug little turd.*

For a moment it seems like me and Dottie and the bus are linked, that none of us could exist without the others. Then there's a faint squeak as Dottie steps on the brakes, and the bus and I begin to slow as we near Ben's driveway.

When I get to school, my best friend, Pilar, says hello by sneaking up behind me and cheerfully hip-checking me away from the locker we both share.

'Where were you last night, Professor?' she asks, pulling out her books. 'I called your house and your cell and no one picked up, *and* I emailed you *and* sent you a text message *and* five IMs.' She takes a deep breath. 'Plus I sent a carrier pigeon, a singing telegram, and a robot.'

Her bangs are cut into a blunt line low across her forehead. The rest of her thick black hair is pulled firmly into a braid that hangs heavy and straight down her back.

'Bad cheese,' I say, ducking down underneath her arms and inserting myself in the exact space she was just in, using my butt to bump her out of my way. 'I spent all night in the bathroom.'

'Gross,' she says, stepping away, and motioning for me to take my sweet time gathering my books. I forget about the bruise on my cheek until Pilar grabs my chin. 'Is that from falling off the can yesterday? Holy crap.'

'I'm all right,' I say, pulling away.

'Whatever you say. So you can still come over to babysit Gracie with me tonight? The professors have one of their special parent-teacher conferences.'

'Totally.' Gracie is Pilar's year-and-a-half-old sister. She was a souvenir from the Midwest, where Pilar and her parents went the summer after our first year of high school. Her parents were teaching a summer program at a college out there, and at the very end of the summer, right before they were supposed to come home, Pilar's mom got pregnant.

Pilar called to tell me that her mom was having a 'tough' pregnancy, and that they'd be staying out there for the whole school year. It was the first time I'd talked to Pilar in weeks, and I cried when she told me she wasn't coming back, not for our entire sophomore year. 'You've

47

barely emailed me or called or anything! And now you're not even coming back?' I had to repeat it two or three times before she could understand, because I was crying so hard. That was the longest year of my entire life, and no matter how much MayBe and even moody Thea tried to include me in everything they did, I could always feel the emptiness of not having Pilar beside me. Sometimes, between Pilar and my dad, I felt like there was more space being taken up by people who weren't there than by the people that actually were.

We're almost to homeroom when a blur of skin-tight jeans and layered flannel hippie skirts comes sliding by us on the linoleum floor.

Its cry, as it passes, sounds something like, 'EEEWWW-UUURRRRLL!'

Pilar and I stop and wait for MayBe (hippie skirts, hemp slippers, beaded necklaces) and Thea (skin-tight jeans, blue Mohawk with rattail) to untangle themselves from each other, and from our homeroom teacher, Mr Mueller, who managed to stop their slide by yelling 'Ack!' and trying to jump out of the way, but not fast enough.

'There's going to be a new girl!' MayBe says.

'Yeah! A new girl's starting tomorrow, or maybe on Thursday,' Thea says. She gasps at my cheek. 'Dude, is that from your face-plant in the bathroom yesterday?'

I shrug her off.

'Ladies,' Mr Mueller warbles, straightening his tie and retaking his station at the classroom door, 'please enter and take your seats.'

When we imitate Mr Mueller, we usually just end up saying 'gobble wobble yobble mobble' because that's what it sounds like when he talks.

'There's a new girl?' Pilar asks him.

'You seem to have that information already,' he warbles.

'Yeah, but what do you *know* about her?' I ask.

'All will be revealed in due time. Please, take your seats.'

We file into the classroom and settle into our usual seats in the back row. The four of us always say that we were alphabetically fated to be friends, from the very first day of kindergarten, when our teacher lined us up next to one another, our first and last names written on stickers in Magic Marker and stuck to our chests.

'Benjamin, Franklin and Cray!' We hear Mr Mueller call from the hallway. 'Please stop pretending to be looking for books in your locker, and come to homeroom!'

A few seconds later Thea's boyfriend, Frank, her brother, Cray, and my neighbour, Ben, walk into the classroom and file into the row in front of ours to take their seats.

'Are they *sauntering*? Oh my God, they're *so* cool,' Pilar whispers to me as the boys take their time getting into their seats. 'Sauntering rocks!' she says loudly enough for the others to hear.

'Eat me,' Frank replies, leaning back in his chair so Thea can lean forward and kiss him. His chair smacks against Pilar's desk.

'With salt!' Pilar says, kicking his chair forward again.

'Neighbour,' Ben says, nodding at me.

Cray sits quietly in his seat, only meeting his sister's eyes for a moment. For as much as they look alike – the stretched-out, lanky frames, the light brown freckles sprayed over their noses and across their cheeks – their personalities are just way different. Thea's all fast-moving parts, and husky laughter, and plans to hitchhike to New York City after high school. She lives with MayBe's family most of the time, sharing MayBe's 'space' behind a Strawberry Shortcake curtain in their giant dome-shaped house that has no walls, and where you are allowed to use only organic bath products because the family uses the old water from the shower to water the vegetable garden.

Thea and MayBe have been best friends forever, just

like Pilar and me. When she was a little kid, Thea tried to be exactly like MayBe. She'd wear MayBe's hippie sundresses and love beads and hand-printed dancing-bear T-shirts. She'd go with MayBe's family to Rainbow Gatherings and full-moon drum circles in the woods, where they'd sleep in teepees, volunteer to peel potatos by the fire pit, and be called 'Little Sister' by all the grown-ups. Pilar and I cried and threw giant day-long hissy fits, begging our parents to let us go too. We wanted to come to school on Monday still smelling like campfire after a weekend away, with cracked and peeling berry-based face paint and singing songs about the earth mother.

One summer there was going to be this giant drum circle at the bottom of the Grand Canyon. MayBe and Thea said thousands and thousands of people were going to go, and that the drums would be so loud you could hear them from the rim of the canyon. There'd be dancing and singing, and cute little babies named Sunflower and Echo whose moms would let Thea and MayBe babysit, strapping the baby to one of their backs in a sling, 'like the native Americans,' MayBe said, 'or like Swedish people.' They were going to sleep in a tent, just the two of them, and they wouldn't have to take a bath for five whole days.

That was the first time I ever felt like I might die of

want. Now I know that I didn't even know what *want* was. Because back then, we still had my dad. I thought that wanting was what Pilar and I did for the weeks before the Grand Canyon drum circle. We would lie on the braided rug in my room, the loose hardwood floor beneath poking into our backs, and we would plot and plan and scheme and declare the general meanness of parents. We would borrow her parents' lab coats and make presentations about the 'Scientific proof that girls who are allowed to go on camping adventures to the Grand Canyon are more likely to succeed than girls stuck on this stupid old mountain for the whole summer.'

MayBe's parents even came over to our house one night, to talk with Mom and Dad, and with Pilar's mom and dad, about why it was perfectly healthy for little girls to run around the woods and dance around campfires. Mom and Dad, though, were not having it. Neither were Pilar's parents. Pilar and I lay on our bellies and listened from the top of the stairs, whispering into the phone to MayBe and Thea, who were at MayBe's house. We still think the deal breaker was the fact that we would have had to poop in the woods. At first I thought that was the part that *really* offended our parents, especially the leaves-as-toilet-paper part.

Of course, it wasn't about the toilet paper. It was about Clarence, and the fact that the sheriff had never caught the Drifter, and I bet Pilar's and my parents were having a hard time letting us out of their sight to go to school, never mind drive three states away in a converted school bus to hang out in the woods with a bunch of grown-up strangers who call themselves Moonbean and Pine Tree.

That's what it came down to. 'How can we see this as an acceptable risk for our children?' Pilar's mom asked MayBe's mom. 'How can the benefits of fresh air and community building outweigh the possible risks of our children being murdered while they sleep?'

MayBe says her parents fought when they came home from our house. They started locking the front door and wouldn't let wandering hippies camp on their land any more. They stopped going to the drum circles and Rainbow Gatherings and put up a gate with a video camera at the end of their long dirt driveway. Sometimes, when we're back in the woods behind MayBe's house, we see other cameras her dad put up, high in trees, their motion detectors set into action by our walking, their one blank eye following us as we move.

MayBe's the only one who kept the flowered dresses

and hemp necklaces. Even her parents, after a while, started to not stand out so much at the grocery store. Thea dresses like me and Pilar, except she chooses fierce high heels over Converse high-tops. Practice, she says, for when she moves to New York, where everyone wears spiked heels, all the time, even to take out the rubbish.

Cray, though, is, like, the absolute absence of energy. He barely talks, or laughs; he barely even *moves*. For some reason he reminds me of oatmeal. Tasteless, lumpy, boring oatmeal. I'm guessing he has some sort of personality that comes out when it's just him and Frank and Ben, because they never complain about the fact that ninety-nine percent of the time he just . . . sits . . . still. Maybe that other one percent of the time he's like an acrobatic circus clown, and that makes it worth it to put up with him.

He never makes eye contact either, which is why the fact that he's pointedly turned around in his seat to stare at me with his stupid expressionless face has made me go cold. He couldn't have seen me last night, in the deputy's truck. It was dark and I turned away from the window to hide my face.

'I heard you rejects f***ed up the Willows sign again last night,' Pilar says to Frank.

Cray raises his eyebrows at me and then turns away.

'Where'd you hear that?' Frank asks, grinning.

Pilar snorts. 'Oh, I'm sorry, was that supposed to be a secret? Maybe you should shut the heck up about it and stop asking everybody if they "saw anything interesting on the way to school this morning". You're so fricking obvious.'

Frank laughs, and then glances at Ben, who's staring hard at him. 'It was a last-minute thing,' Frank says to him in a low voice. 'We'll come get you next time.' He turns and winks at Thea. 'You too, babe.'

'That's not my name,' Thea says, with a glance and a smile at MayBe. 'And don't bother, because I don't want to be a part of it.'

'Seriously, Frank, leave her out of your extra-curriculars,' MayBe says.

Frank ignores her.

'Sure seemed like that was your name yesterday afternoon,' he says to Thea, a not-exactly-friendly smile twitching at his lips. 'And you're already a part of it. And, MayBe,' he says to MayBe with the same twitchy smile and a nod toward Thea, 'she *is* my extracurricular.'

'Dude,' Ben says under his breath, 'really unnecessary.'

'Yeah, jackass,' Pilar says, kicking Frank's chair again, 'totally unnecessary.'

'Hey, Frank,' I say loudly. 'Don't be such a fartknocker, you fartknocker!'

'You guys,' Thea laughs. 'It's fine. He was just joking.'

'He shouldn't talk about you like that, Thea,' MayBe says.

'True,' Pilar and I say in unison.

There's a sort of classroom-wide breath-holding as Thea climbs over her desk and slips on to Frank's lap.

'Oh, Jesus, somebody say something quick so I don't have to hear them kiss!' Pilar practically yells. 'I hate that sound! I hate that sound! It sounds like Dylan eating cereal.'

'Hey!' I say, just as loudly. 'It tastes better when you slurp!'

'I'll say,' Frank groans.

'Oh, holy barf!' Pilar yells.

'Dude.'

We all look to where Cray is still facing toward the front of the classroom.

'Did Cray just say "dude"?' I stage-whisper.

'That's enough, Frank,' Cray says.

'Hey.' Thea stands up. 'You don't get to decide what's enough.'

Cray looks at her. 'That's enough.'

'Shit head,' Thea says, but she doesn't sit back down

with Frank. She squeezes between the desks to sit in her own seat.

I can hear MayBe's whisper as she leans toward Thea. 'Your body is a temple.'

'Shove it,' Thea says, tipping back in her chair.

'Lala!' Grace yells my nickname when I follow Pilar into her house that afternoon. Grace reaches up for me, opening and closing her hands and stomping her pudgy bare feet until I scoop her up and give her perfectly fat cheek a loud kiss. She squirms in my arms and reaches out for Pilar, who holds Grace comfortably in the crook of her left arm, while her right hand runs quickly over Gracie's body like she's checking to make sure it's all still there, finishing by gently touching a finger to Grace's nose.

'Dylan, hello!' Pilar's dad puts his hands on my shoulders and looks into my eyes. 'Are you taking care of your mother? We worry about you, up there all alone.'

Pilar's parents are scientists. Not just scientists but some sort of bigwig scientists who show up in public television documentaries and in scientific journals and newspapers because of the work they're doing to find a way to stop the nasty little beetles that are eating a lot of the trees up-mountain.

'We're OK,' I tell him. And then add, 'We have the Abbotts right down the slope from us.'

'You know what I'd like to do –' he says.

'I like your suspenders,' I say quickly, before he can make me his monthly offer to find my dad and 'bop him one, right on the nose'.

'Why, thank you!' he says, hooking his thumbs under the suspenders and stretching them forward. He's wearing his school suspenders today, which have 'A+' embroidered in different colours all over them. They are the bane of Pilar's existence. Her dad puts his hands back on my shoulders and says, 'If I ever see that old man of yours again, I'm going to pop –'

Pilar puts Grace down and ducks under her dad's arms so she is squeezed between him and me.

'Hello, pumpkin,' her dad says.

'Daddy,' she says pointedly, 'why are you wearing the suspenders?'

'Because you are my A-plus daughter and I want your teachers to know that I know how smart you are.'

She laughs. 'You are an A-plus big dork.' It's weird, being this close to a father-and-daughter moment. We're still pressed against one another, cradled by her dad's arms, so when Pilar leans a tiny bit forward to give her dad a peck on the nose, my body has to shadow hers, and it's like a split-second heartbreak, leaning in to kiss someone who's not there. I step back, out of the circle, and pick Gracie up again. I hold her only for a moment before Pilar's mom comes downstairs and takes her from my arms.

'Dylan,' she says crisply, and I know that's about as much of a greeting as I'm going to get.

'Hello. How are you?' I ask.

Pilar's mom doesn't respond, she just sets Grace down on the floor. Pilar rolls her eyes at me. Her mom's outfit is almost comically the opposite of Pilar's dad's. She's dressed head to toe in black, looking like a big-city art critic, with her artsy, clunky jewellery and owl-eye glasses. I would love to see Pilar's parents at parent-teacher conferences, their version of good cop-bad cop involving her dad's dorky suspenders and her mom's exact and somehow terrifying pronunciation of words like 'potential' and 'institutional inadequacy'.

I love Pilar's house. It's an A-frame like mine, but the first floor is basically just one big wonder of a room, with no walls, the kitchen and dining area and living room just flowing into one another. It feels like the room has taken a really deep breath and stretched out to take a nap. The wood-plank ceiling stretches up fifty feet to the very top of the A, and the side of their house that overlooks the mountains is made entirely of windows.

After Pilar's parents leave, we colour with Grace for a while, and then Pilar takes her upstairs for a nap, switching on the radio on her way back into the kitchen. At Pilar's house it's always either folk or jazz, although occasionally I'll come over and her mom will be dissecting a bug while listening to triumphant metal. This time it's the scratchy recording of a raspy-voiced old man singing about a mountain. Not our mountain, but we know what he means.

'Let's make cookies,' Pilar says.

I wrinkle my nose.

'What?' she asks, laughing.

'I just . . . don't know if I feel like having cookies . . . that you make.'

'Oh, come on!' Pilar says, stamping her foot. 'They'll be fine.'

'All right,' I say, obviously unconvinced.

'You'll see,' she says, in the voice Mom used to use when I'd ask her what Santa had gotten me for Christmas. When she used that voice, it was always something good.

I lean against the counter as Pilar pulls ingredients out of the cabinets. Dry oats, raisins, brown sugar. Brown sugar!

'Oooh!' I say, lunging forward and grabbing the sugar. 'Sweet stuff!'

'I know!' Pilar crows. 'We only have it because it's organic and farmed by minority workers who own shares in the company.'

Usually any sweets we cook at Pilar's house taste suspiciously like something that's good for you and that will 'keep you regular'.

'Yuuuuummmm . . . ,' I say, sticking my finger into the box and licking off the tiny grains. Even though I have a house full of sweets at home, five minutes at Pilar's house and I'm already feeling seriously sugar deprived.

'Are you helping or eating?' she says, handing me a measuring cup.

'Yes,' I say, scooping out the sugar into the bowl, so Pilar can add the other ingredients and mix the batter together.

'OK. Taste this,' she says, holding out a bit of batter on the wooden mixing spoon. 'Sweet, right?'

It has that sort of tame sweetness that every dessert has at Pilar's house, the kind that makes you think, *Maybe I don't actually need to consume eight pounds of sugar every day*. At least, that's what you think till you go home and eat a bowl of pudding and remember how sugar is the best substance on earth.

'It needs chocolate chips and a slab of ice cream, but other than that, it's perfect.'

We spoon the cookies on to the cookie sheet, and Pilar puts them into the oven. I follow her into the living room, and we assume our favourite positions on the couch – feet hanging over the back, heads hovering above the floor. It's getting dusky outside, but we don't turn on the living room light. We like the half dark, Pilar and I.

'Professor,' Pilar says.

'Professor,' I answer.

'Two things,' she says.

'OK. Number one?'

'Number one. What do you think is going on with Thea and Frank?'

'I don't know, but he really pissed me off today in homeroom.'

Pilar laughs. 'I could tell.'

'I just hate the whole thing. The way Frank talks to her, the way Thea so obviously hates it but totally backs down instead of standing up for herself, the way Cray steps in like some hero to get Frank to stop manhandling his sister. I'm sorry, but the whole thing just creeps me out.'

'I'm glad Cray said something,' Pilar says, after a moment. 'Anything to stop the kissing sounds. And she *is* his sister. Frank's lucky Cray didn't bust his stupid blockhead open.'

'Cray would never do that. Frank is, like, his leader.'

'You think?' Pilar says. 'I mean, I know it *seems* like that, and Frank is *totally* Ben's leader, but I feel like Cray maybe just plays along. Like maybe when the three of them are alone, Cray's the one who talks all the time and tells them what to do.'

'What do you think they're up to?'

'You mean with the Willows sign? They've always done crap like that.'

'Yeah, but it seems different now, right? Like, they're always bragging about it, right, but you can tell they keep some stuff secret. Because you know it was them that sugared the gas tank on that tractor at the Willows, right?'

'It totally was them. Idiots.'

'But they didn't tell us. Usually they can't shut up about that stuff, but that time they said nothing.'

'So?'

'So, what if they're going to lead Thea into a life of crime? MayBe will have to bake a nail file into an organic cake so Thea can bust herself out of jail.'

'We'll all have to sit in a car with the lights off outside the jail.'

'Will we have snacks?'

'What?'

'While we're waiting? Can we have snacks? You could bring your oatmeal cookies!'

'Good idea.'

'I'll bring chips, and root beer.'

'And Sour Patch Kids.'

'Correct. So we'll be hunkered down –'

'Hunkered?'

'*Yes*, hunkered down in the car outside the jail –'

'In the total pitch-dark –'

'And then all of a sudden –'

'The search lights will go on, and we'll see scrawny little Thea –'

'Running!' I do an upside-down imitation of a frantic run. 'Across the giant lawn in front of the prison!'

'She'll yell, "Go! Go! Go!"' Pilar laughs. 'And we'll start driving, and then she'll –'

'Cut through the fence with MayBe's nail file –'

'And run alongside the car and –'

'MayBe will hang out the car window and pull Thea in.'

'It'll be awesome,' Pilar says, 'because then we'll totally be outlaws, and we'll have to drive cross-country

64

and be tough girls that solve crimes against women in every town we go to.'

'I was just thinking about that!' I screech. 'We'll be, like, the hottest, brassiest, sassiest, girl gang EVER.'

'Until we get caught.'

'Well, *you're* the one that leaves a trail of green Sour Patch Kids.'

'I hate the green ones,' she says matter-of-factly. 'They taste too green.'

'So we'll be hightailing it across some desert plain, and there'll be, like, fifty cop cars right on our tail.'

'And we won't –,' Pilar says, raising her eyebrows at me.

'We *won't* –' I agree. And then we say together: 'Drive off a cliff.'

'Because we're not going to off ourselves,' Pilar says.

'Just because the world isn't ready for our unstoppable female superpowers.'

'*Thelma & Louise* is, like, the best movie ever,' Pilar sighs. 'Except for the shit box of an ending.'

'And how!' I say in agreement.

We stay upside down, in happy silence for a long while. The sun has started to dip, and in the purpling light I study the thick wooden beams that run crosswise up the slope of the ceiling. If I stare at this certain spot, right between two beams, where nothing else but the white ceiling and brown beams are in my line of vision, it totally feels like I'm floating.

'Wee,' I say.

'Floating?'

'Yep.'

'Professor?' Pilar asks.

'Yes, Professor?'

'Number two.'

'OK, number two.'

'Did you hear about that little girl?' Pilar asks me in a low voice. 'The one from the flatlands who got killed?'

I can feel her looking at me, but I don't turn my head. 'I think I heard something about it on the news this morning. That was all the way in the desert, though, right?'

'It's sort of freaking me out,' she whispers. 'I mean, if anything like that ever happened to Grace . . .'

'Pilar, that was *hours* away from here,' I say, quickly. 'They'll probably catch the guy who did it by the weekend.'

'I've heard that before,' she says darkly. 'That's what they said about the Drifter. They kept saying it was just a matter of time before they caught him, but they never did.

I heard it on the news, you know. They think he's the one who got that little girl in the desert.'

'Wait. Who?' My voice is shaking. What is she talking about?

'The Drifter,' Pilar says. 'They think he's come back and that he's the one who killed that little girl in the desert.'

'Where did you hear that?' I ask. I'm finding it hard to keep my body from going limp, from slipping sideways off the couch into a pile on the floor. Why didn't Deputy Pesquera tell me? Why didn't I know? I think back to my dream, the one I had on the way home from Salvation. The person whose footsteps I could hear behind me. It couldn't be. I would have *felt* it if it were him. Wouldn't I?

'Mom and Dad heard it at the university. Some of their students commute over from Salvation, where it happened.'

'It's not the Drifter,' I say, and even though I mean it to sound reassuring, it just sounds dismissive.

'But what if it is?' Pilar asks, the tightness in her voice a sure sign that she's about to cry. 'What if he's back? I swear to God, Dylan, if he ever came near my Gracie, I'd tear his throat out with my teeth.'

'It's not him!' I finally let my body collapse on to

the floor. I move to my knees, and hold on to the edge of the coffee table, my eyes closed, waiting for my head to stop spinning.

Pilar sits up too. 'They told us they'd catch him, and then they told us he'd never come back. They lied to us, Dylan. Everyone on this mountain is walking around with their eyes closed.'

I open my eyes, and see that she's watching me.

'I'm just . . . ,' I say. 'I don't want it to be him.'

Outside the wall of windows the sun has set, and the darkness has come.

'I should get Grace up or she'll never sleep tonight,' Pilar says, standing. 'Take the cookies out in five minutes, OK?'

I wait till she's upstairs before I go into the downstairs bathroom. I lock the door, and sit on the edge of the tub.

The deputy picks up on the fifth ring. 'Pesquera.'

'Why didn't you tell me?' I ask.

'Dylan?'

I pick a rubber butterfly bath toy up off the floor and squeeze it. It squeaks. I toss it into the tub. 'Last night. W-why didn't you tell me you thought it was him?'

I can hear the creak of her office chair as she stands, and the soft click as she closes her office door.

She clears her throat before she speaks. 'We don't know anything for sure.'

I slide down until I'm sitting on the bath mat and resting my head on my knees. 'But you think it might have been him?'

Deputy Pesquera sighs. 'We're not sure of anything right now, Dylan.'

'But you think it might be . . .'

'You know how this works, Dylan. I can't tell you anything.'

'Oh, but I have to tell you everything?' I ask sharply.

'*Did* you tell me everything?' she asks.

I stand up. 'What is that supposed to mean? Of course I told you everything! I always tell you everything!'

'You call me,' she says, 'if you remember anything else.'

'What did I say in the truck last night, in my sleep?'

She clears her throat again. 'You said, "It's you."'

I listen to the dial tone for a long time before hanging up.

I hear Pilar calling from upstairs, 'Are they out?'

'Yes!' I yell, opening the bathroom door and dashing to the kitchen.

When Pilar comes downstairs, I'm blowing frantically on the cookies before the deep brown on their edges turns black. Pilar hands me a still-sleepy Grace, and starts using the spatula to put the cookies on to a cooling rack.

'I was going to do that,' I say.

'I know,' she says. 'I just . . . I'll do it.'

'Are you all right?' I ask. She doesn't look all right.

'I just got really tired all of a sudden. I don't like the dark,' she says, looking out the window into the early night. 'It makes me think about things. Don't you ever think about things, Dylan? Don't you ever think about Clarence?'

Instead of answering I get soy milk out of the fridge and pour some into a sippy cup for Grace. Pilar hands me a cookie. I sit down with Grace on my lap, her head resting against my shoulder, her breath evening back into sleep.

'Hey, Gracie,' I whisper, breaking the cookie in half and blowing on it till it cools. 'Wake up and eat your cookies. They have a magical ingredient called *sugar*.'

Grace yawns, stretches out her legs, looks at me, and says, 'Lala.'

'I think about Clarence sometimes,' I say to Pilar.

'Me too.'

'It's good, though, to think about him.'

Pilar smiles. 'So we can keep him in our hearts?'

That's what Fran, who was the elementary school

70

secretary when we were in kindergarten, said to us on our first day back to school after Clarence was buried. We all liked her because she would come out and play games with us during recess, and because if she wore her magic snowflake earrings during winter, that meant it was going to snow that day. She changed schools, right along with Pilar's and my class. She was the school secretary for the middle school and is now for the high school. I don't think she could let us go.

'Can we please talk about something else?'

For a second Pilar looks completely deflated, but then she smiles again and says, 'Sure. What'll we do if the nail-file-in-a-cake doesn't work?'

'Hmmm. Smuggle Thea out of prison in a basket of dirty laundry, like in *Annie*?'

When Pilar's parents get home from the conference, the kitchen's been cleaned, dinner is started, and we have Grace painting at the kitchen table.

Pilar's mom insists on paying me, like she always does.

'Really, it's fine,' I say. 'I'm happy to help out.'

'Don't be silly,' her mom says, pushing a ten-dollar bill into my palm with the tips of her blood-red nails. 'Take it!'

She's not a lady I can argue with. I pocket the money,

and pretend to be intensely interested in putting on my book bag as Pilar's mom takes out another ten and tries to hand it to Pilar. 'Here you go, for babysitting.'

'Mom. Don't be ridiculous.'

'Why? You worked as hard as Dylan. You deserve this.'

'I don't need to get paid for being part of this family.'

'Oh, don't be silly.'

Pilar's dad is suddenly just as interested in my book bag. He helps me put it on, and then we make small talk over its uninteresting zipper.

'Family meeting,' Pilar growls, and that's my cue. Just in time, Mom's truck pulls up to the driveway.

'Bye, guys. See you tomorrow, Pilar.'

Pilar's family is big on family meetings. Since she was for most of her life an only child, she and her parents made a lot of decisions by committee. There's never been a lot of 'Because I said so', from her parents. When Grace came along, they all started raising her the same way – by committee, and I know it drives Pilar crazy when her mom tries to treat Pilar like a child, instead of someone with *full voting rights*, as Pilar puts it.

'God, this rain,' Mom says, wiping away condensation from the inside of the windshield with her glove. 'It makes it feel colder than when it actually snows.'

'Mom?'

'The damp, I guess, chills you right to the bone,' she says, taking off her gloves and pressing her hand up close to the heater vent. 'I can't wait for first snow.'

'Mom?'

'Hm?'

'When the deputy briefed you on what happened, on that girl in Salvation, what did she say?'

Mom puts the truck into reverse and pulls out on to the street. We're back on Lakeshore Drive before she answers me.

'Let's see,' she says. 'She told me basically the same thing you told me. That you had a vision of the little girl being trapped inside a barrel. A blue barrel, out behind their little downtown area. She told me you two almost got in a wreck, which I didn't like hearing about.'

'Did she say anything else? About who did it?'

'Nope. Why do you ask?'

'They just haven't caught him yet,' I say. 'And I wish they would.'

'Oh, they'll catch whoever did it, baby. They always do.'

'They didn't catch the Drifter,' I answer.

'You kids still call him that?' she asks.

73

I shrug. 'What else should we call him?'

'Long gone,' Mom says. 'You should call him Long Gone and Never Coming Back.'

'Are you talking about the Drifter or Dad?'

She doesn't look at me, just makes a shocked sound in her throat that sounds like 'Oh'.

'Because Dad's not coming back, is he?'

Mom fiddles with the heating vent. 'I don't know.'

'Yes, you do,' I say. 'You know he's not coming back. We don't even know where he lives.'

'He knows where *we* live,' she says sharply.

Sometimes I forget that my mom must still love him. Sometimes I even forget that I'm the reason he left.

The night my dad didn't come home after work was three days after my ninth birthday, and three days after I had a vision of the very last moments of a little kid named Wesley's life. I didn't know it then, but that ended up being the first vision that my dad ever knew about. Mom and I ate meat loaf at the table alone together, with the phone sitting next to her plate. I said, 'Mommy, you know he really likes your meat loaf, right?' I said it ten different ways, so scared that her feelings were hurt and thinking of what I'd say to my dad when he got home. She kept saying,

'Oh, I know.' Like they were playing a joke on me together. I let myself think he was out getting a late birthday present for me. A pony that I could keep at Ben's, most likely.

After dinner Mom let me watch a movie while she made another round of calls to his cell phone, his office, his boss, and his friends, anywhere she could think of. By eight o'clock I could tell she was really worried. We kept the phone on the counter in the bathroom while I took my bath. She let me sleep in her room that night.

Sheriff Dean was on our couch, across from Mom in her armchair, when I came downstairs in the morning. For a second, from behind, I thought he was Dad. Sheriff Dean is bald, and the first thing I thought was that Dad had gotten cancer and lost his hair overnight. I scrambled over the back of the couch on to Sheriff Dean's lap, yelling, 'Dad!'

Sheriff Dean jumped out from under me, holding me by my shoulders and pushing me away, hard. I don't know what made me cry more – that he wasn't my dad or that he'd handled me so roughly. It was the first time I'd ever felt how strong grown-ups were, compared to little kids, and it'd scared me half to death. Sheriff Dean didn't handle it too well either. His hand was over his heart now, his other hand on the butt of his gun, like it might fly out of its holster. 'Dylan! You don't jump on someone who has a gun!' His booming voice made me cry even harder. Mom picked me up off the couch and held me. I clung tight to her neck, tighter still when Sheriff Dean leaned forward to say softly, 'I'm sorry I shouted, Dylan. I just got scared you'd get hurt.'

I always liked Sheriff Dean and hated the way flat-landers treated him like a walk-around character at an amusement park. His pudgy belly, good manners, and the fact that everyone called him 'Sheriff Dean' made the weekenders get all cackle-laugh and say, 'Bryce, get the camera and take my picture with the long arm of the law.' They'd think he was really charming, until one of their mini-mansions got vandalised. Then they'd insult him while he took the police report, and usually call the down-the-hill police to see if they would take care of it. That's why they wanted all their mini-mansions to be behind a gate, so they could hire their own security detail.

Mom was holding me against her, stroking my hair. She was crying, and at first I thought it was because Sheriff Dean had yelled at me. I looked at him and thought, *Boy, are you gonna get it*. But she didn't yell back at him or kick him out of the house. She sat down in the armchair and pulled me on to her lap. I let my body go slack against her, my back snug in the warm triangle of space between her ribs and arm.

'And he didn't call last night?'

Mom shook her head. 'I spoke with him at lunch and asked him to pick up ketchup for the meat loaf at the market on his way home.'

'At Sheboa's?'

'Oh,' Mom said, looking helplessly at Sheriff Dean. 'I didn't tell him where. Just asked him to pick it up.'

Dean nodded and said, 'We've contacted the boys down the hill. Maria, I think we should make an announcement. Ask folks if anyone's seen anything.'

Mom started crying harder, shaking her head. 'It's a small mountain, Dean. I've made calls, and everyone knows he's missing.'

'Still, Maria, I think a press conference might do some good.'

Mom sniffed. 'OK.'

Sheriff Dean stood. 'I'll set it up. Can Sarah Abbott come stay here with you?'

Sarah Abbott, I knew, was Ben's mom.

Mom nodded. 'I've called her already. She'll be here soon.'

I stayed home from school that day. Dottie came by after she'd dropped all the kids off at school. She just showed up at the door. She sat me down to colour at the kitchen table while Mom was in the living room with Ben's mom. Dottie even made lunch for us all, though Mom barely ate anything. At one-thirty Dottie said she had to go, and Mom took me upstairs so I could have a nap.

Mom was on the phone with the sheriff when I woke up and came back downstairs. My dad was not on the couch. Mom was looking with scared eyes at Ben's mom and saying into the phone, 'Why do you need that? Sheriff Dean, you tell me right now why you need that.'

Mom flipped through our address book with a shaky hand. 'It's Dr Wigham,' she said, 'but that's a damn scary piece of information to ask me, even as a precaution, and you know it.'

Dr Wigham was our dentist. I imagined my dad having a mouth full of cavities, too afraid to come home and face Mom.

The next day Dr Wigham was one of the people standing behind Mom, along with Sheriff Dean and Deputy Pesquera, when Mom gave a press conference on our front steps. She held me in her arms. TV reporters from down the hill were there, and their microphones hovered like a swarm of metal bees in front of Mom's face. I closed my eyes and hid my face against her shoulder so I wouldn't see them sting her.

She told the bees she missed my dad and wanted him to come home. She said, 'And if anybody knows where he is, they should call . . . They should call . . .' Before we'd gone outside, Sheriff Dean had written a telephone number down for my mom, so she could read it out loud to the bees. But instead of reading the number from the paper crumpled in her hand, my mom froze.

'Five-five-five . . . ,' I said, and the metal bees all turned their heads and crept closer to my mouth. One of the soggy-shoed reporters said, 'What did you say, honey?' And I said slowly, so they would be sure to hear it, 'Five-five-five-three-four-five-eight.'

Then Sheriff Dean stepped in and said a few words, and we all filed back into the house, the reporters outside filming intros that all sounded like, 'Where is Martin Moran? The Pine Mountain man disappeared two days ago . . .'

Deputy Pesquera went into the kitchen to make coffee for the grown-ups, and hot chocolate for me. Mom set me in the armchair and tucked a blanket around me, telling me to close my eyes for a little bit. She sat on the couch and pushed her palms against her face. Sheriff Dean sat next to her and patted her back, making soothing noises. Dr Wigham paced behind the couch. He'd been there since early in the morning, cutting his vacation short to bring us pictures of my dad's teeth from his office. Every time the phone rang, Dr Wigham would pick up the file with my dad's name on it, looking like he was ready to dash out the door. I didn't know what the pictures were for, and no one would tell me. In the kitchen Officer Pesquera was talking quietly to someone on our phone. She hung up and signalled something to Sheriff Dean.

'Maria,' he said to Mom. Mom looked at him and then at Officer Pesquera.

'Who were you on the phone with?' Mom's voice was shaking. 'Who were you just talking to?'

'Maria,' Sheriff Dean said slowly, in the way he would talk to our class about stranger danger. 'They found his car.' Dr Wigham stopped pacing. 'At the bottom of the hill. It's been burned, stripped. There was some blood, Maria.' Mom sobbed, pulling me out from the chair and sitting back on the couch with me, saying, 'Oh God, oh God, oh God. Was it his? Was it his blood?'

'We don't have a DNA match yet, but it does not look good.'

Then the telephone rang, and Dr Wigham leaned over the couch with my dad's file and held it in front of Sheriff Dean's face as the sheriff reached for the phone. Mom yelled, 'Damn it, Wigham!' and grabbed the file and pitched it across the room, where the black-and-white shiny translucent pictures of my dad's teeth scattered across the floor. The phone was still ringing and Mom grabbed it out of Sheriff Dean's hand.

'Hello?' she said, and her voice was like a string pulled tight. She looked at Sheriff Dean, her eyes wide, the colour gone from her face.

'Martin?' she said, her voice shaking. And then she screamed, 'Martin! Where are you? Are you OK?'

There was a pause as she listened, her brow furrowed. 'A note?' she asked.

Dr Wigham was across the room, stooped over and gathering the photos. He stood up, holding a piece of paper, and said, 'This note? It was under the coffee table.' He started to read the note out loud, even as he handed it to Mom. 'My darling Maria,' he read, before Mom grabbed it out of his hand, her wild eyes scanning it like she could read it all at once.

'My *darling Maria*,' she said, her words running into one another. '*As I write this, you are curled around Dylan in her bed. She had a nightmare last night, and you went into her room and held her until you both slept. I looked in on you this morning, at the way Dylan's head was tucked under your chin, at the way her back pressed against your stomach, your arms slung around her middle, her thumb stuck firmly in her mouth. You are the two most beautiful creatures I have ever laid eyes on, and that is how I want to remember you. I have started this letter a thousand times, but there is no easy way to say what I have to say.*'

Mom stopped reading out loud, her voice lowering to a wordless murmur as she read the next lines.

'You're leaving us?' she screamed into the phone.

That scream was like a sharp knife, lopping off a part of my body that I couldn't even see, that I didn't even realise was there until it was gone. By now, though, all these years later, you can barely even tell I'm limping.

The dream comes again and I find myself standing in the moonlit desert, the cool air pushing through the fabric of my sweatshirt, the low buildings of downtown Salvation outlined in the distance against the night sky. The hole in front of me is dark. I'm standing too close to its edge, and

I step back, knocking into the blue plastic barrel. I don't want to touch it, but I have to hold on to it to steady myself, to keep from stumbling, from falling into the hole. The wind dies down and I hear the footsteps again, rushing up behind me. *Who are you?* I ask in the dream, my hand still on the barrel, my heartbeats tripping over themselves, pounding against my chest. I turn around again and again, but I end up looking in the same direction, the footsteps behind me again, coming closer. *Wake up*, I say, *wake up, wake up, wake up.*

A chill draft licks at my cheeks and the tips of my earlobes, and I snuggle more deeply into the warmth of my bed, peeking out from under the covers to see if I've left my window open. The window is closed, but the air in my room has gone frigid, its moist chill as sudden and sharp as stepping outside in just pyjamas to see a snow-storm. I pull the blankets up over my head, letting my breath warm my face, and vowing once again to convince my mom that we need central heating – floor vents that, like in Pilar's house, gust out floods of hot air. I kick my feet, trying to warm the cold sheets. My right foot bumps up against something. Am I really scrunched that far down? Far enough to kick the bed frame? I keep my head under the blankets, lifting them from underneath, until in the murky darkness I can see my foot resting against the underside of a blanket that is pinned from above, by something that is definitely not my bed frame.

'MOM!'

I play ostrich for the ten seconds it takes her to dash into my room and tear the covers off me. She finds me curled in a ball, my eyes squeezed shut, and my fingers in my ears. I open one eye wide enough to make sure it's her, and the other wide enough to make sure there's no monster sitting at the foot of my bed, and I sit up.

'I had a nightmare.'

Mom yawns. 'I'd say so. What about?'

I shrug, now convinced that it really was my bed frame that my foot bumped against. 'Monsters?'

She pulls the covers back over me. 'It's freezing in here.' I lie back down, pulling the blankets to my chin. Mom sits on the edge of the bed, and yawns again. 'Are you sure it was about monsters?' she asks. 'It wasn't about Tessa?'

'I don't dream about Tessa,' I lie. 'I don't dream about any of them.'

She nods.

'You know that,' I say, more harshly than I mean to.

What I want to say is, *You're the reason I don't dream about them. I block them out, for you.*

My mom studies me. 'What if you did dream about them?'

'What do you mean?'

'What do you think you would see?'

'I don't know.' I close my eyes, faking sleepiness. 'Probably the same thing I saw the first time.'

'Probably,' my mom says. 'You're probably right.'

3

I feel like I'm being flooded.

A secret can do that to you.

It can spend weeks and months and years shrunk down so small it's just a warm knot at the base of your spine, and then all of a sudden it can gush up, like a tide rising and pulsing against the inside of your skin, and while everyone else is taking notes in last-period geometry, it's all you can do to keep from drowning right there in your high-tops.

'Are you all right?' Pilar whispers to me when I stand up from my desk.

I try for an unconcerned nod, but end up just sticking out my bottom lip and making some sort of wobbly bobble-head motion.

Pilar laughs.

More than anything in the whole entire world, I want to sit back down at the desk with her and laugh so hard that we get kicked out of class. I want the ridiculous head bobble that I just did to get entered into the Pilar and Dylan Stupid Faces Hall of Fame, for us to make at each other in really inappropriate moments. Like during church. Or in one of those assemblies where storytellers in rainbow leotards come to 'rap' to us about the dangers of drugs and drinking.

When I get to the front of the classroom, I stop. Our teacher, Mrs Gunther, turns to me from the dry-erase board, pausing mid-isosceles triangle, and says, 'Ms Driscoll?'

I make a sound like 'Arnrng!' my hand pressed to my stomach, my tongue halfway out of my mouth.

She reels back ever so slightly and points at the door with her dry-erase marker.

'Well, go, then!'

I run out into the hall and bend over double with laughter that turns quickly to tears, my shoulder pressed against the wall to keep myself from falling over.

I stand up straight and wipe my face with my T-shirt and take deep breaths until they stop getting caught in my throat.

'I'm a mess,' I say aloud, laughing. Then crying. And then hiccuping so hard I burp. Which makes me laugh.

I peek out the window and see the buses have arrived,

and that the bus drivers have gone inside the cafeteria for coffee. I slip out the side door.

The school bell rings and I stay lying down where I've hidden on the bus, scrunching myself a little to make sure my head isn't hanging out into the aisle. I hear the voices of the bus drivers coming toward the bus. Dottie curses when she gets to the bus, seeing the bus door I left open. She climbs into the driver's seat, and in a moment the lights flicker on and warm, dry air comes gushing out of the heater vents.

The intercom crackles before Dottie's voice comes booming through the speakers. 'Fran saw you get on the bus, so you might as well sit up.'

For a second I have the irrational hope that there's some other kid slouched down in another seat, maybe all the way in the back of the bus.

'Oh, for Pete's sake,' Dottie's voice crackles. 'Dylan, sit up.'

I push myself upright, peeking over the tops of the seats to see Dottie looking at me in the oversize rear-view mirror.

'You all right?' she asks, putting the microphone away.

I nod.

'Fran wants me to make sure you're not on drugs. Are you on drugs?'

I shake my head.

'Say something so I know you're not on drugs.'

'I'm not on drugs,' I say, sitting up taller.

'OK, then.' She picks up the microphone again and turns the channel. 'She's fine, Fran. I think she just missed me.' They both laugh, Fran's voice tinny and snapping.

The wind off the lake is whipping sand against the side of the bus. The sound makes me think of buckshot, or the way Mom makes popcorn kernels clattering into the heavy iron pot she made my dad carry with them on the bus all the way cross-country, when they were just married and in love and still together. It makes me think of the night, in the desert, the truck's dizzying spin sending sand into the air, and the sound of it falling back down again.

I lean out the window of the bus, keeping my mouth closed and my eyes squeezed shut against the grit peppering my face. I could let the wind and the sand work their work on me, teasing at my skin, until it starts to crack and break off and fly away, until I have no face, and then no head, and then no me. I'll just be sand, blowing through the pine trees until the wind runs out of breath and all the pieces of me fall to the ground. My problems couldn't follow me. They'd get snagged in the sharp branches of the tallest trees, where they would flutter and snap in the wind like grey ghosts.

'Bad cheese again?'

I open my eyes. Pilar is looking up at me from the sidewalk. She reaches up to hand me the geometry notebook I left in class. 'MayBe thinks you're lactose intolerant.'

'That could be it,' I say.

'And Thea thinks you're faking it,' she snorts.

'I'm not faking.'

'She just wants to know how you do it so well.'

The wind picks up and we both raise a hand to shield our faces.

'I'm not –'

'So, I take it you're not coming with us over to Thea's so she can practice on your hair?' Pilar interrupts. I'd forgotten. Thea's mom said she'd give her a job at the salon this summer, if Thea got good enough.

'My stomach –'

'Hurts again. I know,' Pilar says.

She scuffs the pavement with a black high-top, and I follow her gaze to where MayBe and Thea are walking out of school. They wave to us, and Pilar points to me and makes a barfing motion. 'Feel better!' they call.

'It's all right,' Pilar says. 'We'll do it tomorrow if you're better. OK, then.' Pilar pauses, and then looks up at me. 'Well, get well soon.'

She steps back from the bus.

'Pilar, come on, I'm sorry,' I say, leaning further out the window. 'Please don't be mad at me.'

'I'm not mad at you,' she says. 'I just wish you'd feel better already.'

'I will,' I say quickly. 'I'm sure I'll feel better soon.'

'Go home and drink some ginger tea or something,'

The bus rumbles to life with the last of the students trailing on, and I pull myself back inside. 'You still love me, though, right?' I call out the window.

'Like the sister I never wanted,' she says. She runs for her bus and calls back over her shoulder, 'Call me after you puke or poop or whatever it is you need to do.'

'OK!' I shout. 'I will! Bye!' I close the window, collapse against the seat, and wipe the dirt away from the corners of my mouth and eyes.

The rain has started again, and Dottie has turned on her windshield wipers. I rub a line into the steam that's gathered on the window and then touch my chilled finger to my bruised cheek.

In the village the school bus stops in front of the grocery store with its vinyl banner strung up across the front, reading *New Management!* There's a bunch of construction workers standing outside of the store's giant new front window, and as I walk up to the front of the bus, I stoop a little to try to see out the windows. I get to the front just in time to hear Dottie's shocked whisper: 'Those dirty sons of buttercups!'

'What's going on?' I ask, and she shifts her position so I can see out her driver's side window. The workers have ripped off the letters that have, for as long as I've lived here, spelled out *Sheboa's Grocery*. They've even pried off the giant lopsided wooden cut-out of a pine tree that used to tower over the letter *S*. The new sign, laid out on the ground in the rain, reads *Paradise Mountain Gourmet Grocery* in fancy script, punctuated by a perfectly straight drawing of a pine tree.

Dottie's already on the radio, barely bothering to open the bus door for us, saying into the receiver, 'Frannie, you'll never guess where I *won't* be buying my groceries from now on.'

When I get off the bus, I see the weekend bumper sticker war has already started. In the parking lot in front of the grocery store, there's a sports car with a bright yellow bumper sticker that reads *If you didn't want us up here, why'd you call it Paradise?*

92

'We were outvoted,' I say to myself, weaving through the small crowd of locals who have gathered in the rain to curse the new sign.

'You got that right,' one of them says as I walk by.

'Like to see that little whippet try to drive down the hill in this rain.'

'Robbie, you'll be towing them up over the side before the weekend's out, I guarantee it.'

I turn and see that Frank's dad is in the crowd, laughing from under the brim of his grease-stained baseball cap. 'You gonna drum up some business for me?' he asks the man who just spoke. 'Give that hot rod a little nudge toward the guardrail?' Everyone laughs.

I walk away from the crowd and step into the narrow alley that runs between Mountain Candy and the pharmacy and leads to the back parking lot, where I can get to the police station's side door without being seen. The space is tight enough that I have to walk almost sideways, my shoulders rubbing against the brown-shingled walls.

I come out of the other side of the alley to the narrow dirt parking lot that separates the buildings from the forest. Most of the people who work in the stores park back here, freeing up parking spaces out front for the

93

weekenders. I walk quickly down the line of cars until I come to the end of the last building. I peek around the corner and then hurry down the side to reach a set of metal stairs that are just out of sight of the front sidewalk. I take them two at a time, yank open the door, and almost trample a girl my age who's trying to walk out.

She looks me full in the face and gives me a wide smile, like we're long-lost friends, like we've just been reunited and we're studying each other's faces to see what's changed.

'Sorry,' I mumble, stepping aside so she can get through the door.

'That's OK,' she says, still studying me as she passes. She pauses for a moment when we're face-to-face, her smile exaggerating the sharp point of her chin.

I step further out of the way, but she doesn't move. I clear my throat and say, 'OK, then.'

She nods, still staring at me, and finally starts down the steps. I let the glass door close behind me, and watch the girl walk down. I look quickly away when she turns and smiles at me.

'Friendly people freak me out,' I say, walking over to where Lucy Barrett, my childhood babysitter, sits reading behind the reception desk.

'She was just being friendly,' Lucy says, absently, turning a page in her romance novel.

'Exactly. Freaky. What are you reading?' I ask, walking over to the desk and resting my chin on its high counter. Lucy's got a wet chunk of her hair stuck to her cheek. Lucy has always chewed her hair, especially when she's reading romance. Pilar and I stole one of her books once, when Lucy babysat for us. The book was called *Forbidden Lust*, and we took turns with MayBe and Thea reading it out loud to one another at slumber parties.

Lucy closes her book, placing it cover-side-down on the desk. 'I'm not reading anything. And that friendly freak of a girl is going to be starting at your school in the next couple of days.'

'No way!' I say, looking back toward the door. 'That was the new girl?'

'Yep.'

My excitement at being the first one of my friends to see her disappears when I realise that when the new girl sees me at school, she'll probably mention seeing me here, at the police station. I'll need to make up a lie.

'Say you're picking up a wood-burning permit for your mom,' Lucy says.

I look at her. When Lucy started working at the

station, I made Deputy Pesquera promise that she wouldn't tell Lucy about me.

'Look,' Lucy says, exasperated. 'I don't know why you're here, and I don't care. It's obvious *you* care, though, so just tell the new girl you were here picking something up for your mom. Does it have something to do with the bruise on your cheek? Because I'm not above kicking someone's ass for you. Are you here for Deputy Pesquera?'

I nod.

'She's out, but should be back soon. Do you want to see Sheriff Dean instead?'

'That's OK, I'll wait. Did you see that bullshit going on in front of Sheboa's?'

'Watch your language, and yes, I saw it.'

'You don't think it's bull . . . crap?'

'Weekenders spend money, Dylan,' Lucy says with a sigh. 'And they're more likely to spend their money in a place called Paradise than a place called Pine Mountain.' She draws out the *i* in 'pine', imitating the flat-sounding vowels that the old mountain folks have. 'That's why the new name passed, because lots of people up here have no other way to make money except from the weekenders.'

'I guess. It's still bullshit. They're not supposed to change the name till January.'

The front door of the station opens and Deputy Pesquera walks in.

'Lucy,' she says.

'Dylan's here to see you,' Lucy says, as if the deputy couldn't see me for herself.

'Come on back.'

I follow Pesquera through the heavy glass-and-metal door that separates the reception area from the main part of the station.

When we get to her office, she sets her hat on top of the computer printer and sits heavily in her chair.

I sit in the chair across from her.

'So, what can I do for you?' she asks me.

'Did you find anything out?'

'About what?'

'About who it was who killed that girl.'

'Nothing conclusive.'

'Nothing conclusive,' I mimic. 'But you think it might have been . . .'

'Dylan, what are you doing here?'

I look away from her heavy stare. 'What is that?' I ask, standing and walking to the map hanging on her wall. 'When did you put this up?'

She doesn't answer. She just sighs, gets up, closes the

97

office door, and walks over to where I'm standing. The deputy towers over me, the elbows of her crossed arms even with my ears.

The map is of the mountain and of the flatlands below. There are two pins stuck into it.

'This is where we were the other night?' I ask, pointing to the red pin set into the desert.

She nods down at me.

'And this blue one's in the woods outside the village, where they found Clarence.'

She nods again.

I press a finger next to the pin in the desert and stretch out my hand until it reaches the pin in the village.

'You think he's coming back,' I say, looking at the small bowl full of tacks sitting on the bookshelf below the map.

'Let me show you something.' I follow the deputy back to her desk and watch as she opens the top drawer. She looks at me. 'I'm not supposed to show you this.' She pulls out a large plastic evidence bag. At first I think it's empty, until she holds it out for me to see, her large knuckles gripping the top of the bag.

'What is that?' I ask, peering at the tiny shreds caught in one corner of the bag. They look like tiny wood shavings, except made out of metal.

'Do they mean anything to you?' she asks.

I shake my head.

'Look harder,' she says, holding the bag closer to me. The thin shreds are curled around one another, some of them corkscrew-shaped, others in the shape of Cs or Ss.

'Where did you find these?' I ask.

'In Clarence's hair,' she answers, dropping the bag back into her drawer. I sit down heavily in the chair next to the desk, painfully bumping my hip on the chair arm as I do.

'I think I'm going to be sick,' I say, rolling forward so my palms are pressed against the linoleum floor. I close my eyes to keep the view of my sneakers from swirling in front of me.

I hear the deputy step closer, and open my eyes to see she's set the wastebasket next to me.

'Why did you show me that?'

'They found the same sort of metal shavings in the barrel with Tessa. They look like a match. And what I need' – she crouches down in front of me – 'is for you to think back to the other night, and to Clarence, and see if you can remember anything.'

'But I can't,' I say quickly. 'I told you everything I saw.'

'I know you did,' she says, 'but maybe you can

think back. Maybe there's something you missed.'

'There's not.' I try to keep the growing panic out of my voice. 'There's never anything different, just what I saw the first time.'

She can't hide the disappointment in her face.

'I'm s-sorry,' I stammer, a familiar hotness creeping up my neck. 'I'm really sorry.'

The deputy pulls a tissue from the box on her desk and hands it to me. 'It's all right. I shouldn't have asked you that. You'll be hearing a lot about those shavings. In the next couple of days we're doing a joint press release with Salvation. Until then, keep it to yourself.'

'OK.'

'You want a ride home?'

'No, thanks. I'll call Mom from the library.'

Great. I'm just coming out of the driveway between the police station and the post office when Frank's truck rumbles to a stop in the street in front of me. Next to Frank is Thea, and sandwiched next to her are Ben and Cray. Frank says something to Thea, and she shrugs. Cray opens the passenger-side door without saying anything, and I grab his outstretched hand and get in, climbing over him and Ben so I can sit in Thea's lap.

'Hey, neighbour,' Ben says. 'How's that belly?'

'It's all right,' I say, bracing myself with a palm against the peeling roof of the truck as we start bumping down the road. 'Frank, you need new shocks.'

'You and Pilar have a fight?' Thea asks.

'Nope. I just had to come to town before I went home.'

'But I thought your stomach . . .'

'Nope. I'm fine. I had to pick something up for my mom, that's why I couldn't go to Pilar's.'

'Whatever.' Thea snorts.

'We're taking a shortcut,' Frank says.

Thea slips an arm around my waist, and we all sway to the side as Frank pulls sharply off of Lakeshore Drive and on to the trail that runs up the mountain to Ben's house. When we come out of the woods into the small field above Ben's barn, Frank stops the truck. Cray opens the door and looks at me. I look at Ben. 'Aren't you going home?'

Ben shakes his head.

'Yeah, he is. We're running an errand,' Frank says. 'He doesn't want to come. Neither do you.'

Cray opens the door further.

'Come on, neighbour,' I say, trying to laugh. 'I know when we're not wanted.'

I climb over Ben and Cray and out of the truck. I can't hear what the low conversation is that Ben's having with

Frank, but I can tell neither one of them is happy about it. Ben finally gets out of the truck, and Frank starts driving before Cray even has the door closed.

We watch the tail lights disappear into the forest. I look up the trail that cuts through the woods from Ben's, and see the dark outline of my house, and wish that its black windows were glowing with the warm lamplight that would mean my mom was home. Instead the house stands dark and uninviting.

'You want help with the horses?' I ask.

Ben's still staring at the tracks left by Frank's truck. He finally sighs and grins at me. 'Sure. Thanks.'

'Hey, Toots,' Mom says from the kitchen when I walk into the house an hour later. 'It's dark out; I was getting worried.'

'I'm sorry,' I say, dropping my bag and jacket on to the couch in front of the fireplace and going into the bathroom to wash the dirt from my hands. I can smell chicken baking. I'm starving. 'I was helping Ben with the horses.'

'That was nice of you.'

'Who's the message from?' I ask, eyeing the blinking red light on the phone.

'Your Aunt Ruby.' Mom opens the oven and pokes at the chicken with a fork.

'Again? Why's she stalking us?'

'Don't talk about your aunt that way. And I don't know why she's stalking us. Damn it!' she yells, running to the sink and putting her hand under cold water. 'I burned myself.'

I'm already at the freezer, wrapping ice cubes in a dish towel.

We eat dinner in front of the TV, trying not to spill rice on the old quilt that covers us both. The angry red blotch on Mom's thumb fades to a muted pink, and the uneasiness inside of me settles with the sound of Mom laughing at dumb jokes on the television.

'I've got homework,' I say. 'I'm going upstairs.'

I call Pilar.

'I'm better!' I say as soon as she picks up the phone.

4

'You had a lot going on last night,' Mom says when she comes in from her run the next morning. I'm curled under the afghan on the couch, slurping a bowl of chocolate cereal and watching one of those really perky morning-show ladies interviewing a puff-haired woman who has a really appealing snaggle tooth. 'How long have you been up?'

I shrug. 'I got up right after you left. Did you know this show is on for, like, three hours every morning? It's called *Good Morning, Sunshine!* and they do the local news and weather every ten minutes, and in between they do cooking and fashion shows and interviews. This lady here,' I say, pointing to the snaggletooth, 'works for *Celebrity!* magazine and she's giving the weekly "Hooked Up, Shacked up, Knocked Up, Broken Up" update. It's all about what celebrities are –'

'I get it,' Mom says.

What I don't say is that I've been watching to see if

the local news mentions the metal shavings found in Salvation.

Mom sits down next to me on the couch and unties her sneakers. 'That host bugs me. Too perky.'

'She's not so bad,' I say. Maybe it's the lack of sleep, but I'd actually started to laugh at the host's dumb jokes.

'Were you having nightmares last night?' Mom asks.

I drink the chocolatey milk from the bowl and keep my eyes on the TV. 'Nope,' I lie. 'Why? Was I talking?'

She laughs. 'No more than usual. You've always been a jabber-jaw in your sleep.'

Then why can't I ever remember dreaming?

'What'd I say?'

'I don't remember,' she says, getting up. 'I'm going to go stretch and shower.'

'I'm going to watch the news and the weather' – I glance at the clock – 'three more times, and in between I'm going to learn how to set a gorgeous Thanksgiving table, improve my credit, and find out if my kids are smoking weed. And then I'm going to school.'

'You might want to get dressed first,' she says on her way upstairs.

Aunt Ruby calls when Mom is in the shower, and I watch the Thanksgiving segment on mute while I talk to her. The cereal's made me hyper, made me brave.

'Auntie, why are you calling so much all of a sudden?'

'Ask your mama,' she answers.

'I did. She says she doesn't know.'

'Your mama lies,' she says, stretching out the word 'lies'.

I'm speechless for a second. Does the fact that she's Mom's sister trump the 'nobody talks bad about my mama' rule? I decide that even if it doesn't, I'll let it go because I actually like talking to Aunt Ruby.

'So, what are you doing today, Auntie?' I ask.

'Ohhh, nothing, nothing at all. I'm going to sit here on the porch, and then I might take a walk after it rains, find some worms, go fishing, and catch dinner in the river.'

'That sounds nice,' I say, turning off the TV. 'Did Mom fish when she was a kid?'

'Oh, your mama loved to go fishing,' Aunt Ruby says, laughing. 'And when I was a little girl, she'd hold my hand all the way down the river, and put those squirmy worms on the hook for me.'

'Did Aunt Peg come?'

'She did,' Aunt Ruby answers, 'but she didn't fish. She liked to sit and read out loud to us while we fished.'

I can picture them, three little girls in pretty dresses

sitting in the sun on the weedy green banks of a river, feet dangling into the water.

'Would you bring snacks?' I ask. Descriptions of food are always my favourite part of a story. I'm wondering if Mom and her sisters brought theirs down to the river in a bucket, like Laura Ingalls Wilder did in the *Little House on the Prairie* books.

My aunt laughs. 'We did, we did, but we carried our snacks in brown paper bags, and since we also carried the *worms* in brown paper sacks, sometimes your aunt Peg would get confused while she was reading and reach her hand into the bag and get a wiggly, sticky surprise.'

I laugh. 'You would switch the bags?'

'Only when she wasn't looking,' she says, and laughs.

'That's funny.'

'Oh, it was just silly fun. That was a long time ago.'

'It's still like that where you live, though, isn't it? Sort of peaceful and quiet?'

'You have your mama bring you out here so you can see for yourself. You need to meet your people, Dylan.'

'I met you guys,' I say, 'when Great-grandmama died.'

'You call that pit stop a visit? No, you need to come and set at my kitchen table and tell me about your friends while I make you some of my famous fruit salad.'

'Then can we sit on the porch and snap beans?'

She laughs. 'Sure we can. I buy my beans at the grocery, but if you want to snap them in half, you're welcome to it.'

'Thanks,' I say, embarrassed by my front-porch country fantasy. I can't help it. Mom's stories about being a little girl sound even better than *Little House on the Prairie* to me.

'Tell your mama to call her sister,' Aunt Ruby says, and then I'm talking to the dial tone.

'Who was that?' Mom asks, coming back downstairs in her work clothes.

'Who do you think?'

'What'd she say?'

'For you to call her.'

'I bet she did. You should go get changed for school.'

Great-grandmama was ninety-eight when we went to visit. She was in a nursing home already by then, close to the house my mom grew up in, where Peg and Ruby and my grandma still live. It wasn't just me and Mom and my dad who came to visit, it was all the Driscolls, from everywhere. Everyone was greats and seconds – great aunts, great-uncles, second cousins, second cousins twice removed.

We went to the nursing home as soon as we pulled

into town, because *It was serious*, according to Mom and Dad's whispered conversations in the front seat of the car. Everyone was there already, in Great-grandmama's room and spilling out into the hall. My dad carried me at first, in through the front door, and then Mom took me, and I could feel her chest swell, her spine straighten, as we approached the relatives standing outside my great-grandmama's room. It was the most special I'd ever felt. As we approached, everyone stopped talking, they stopped moving, they just stopped and looked. Since I wasn't exactly a little Gerber baby, I was totally unused to this reaction. Usually grown-ups shook my hand and made a joke about me looking like the tax collector. But these grown-ups looked into my face and smiled.

As Mom carried me into the room, the crowd around Great-grandmama's bed parted, and Mom held me tighter as she stood next to where my great-grandmother lay. I remember thinking, *Wow, that is one old lady*. A face that made you think of a raisin, or a finger kept in the bathtub too long. But even under the wrinkles, there was the cleft of her chin, there were her wide-set eyes.

The old lady looked at me, and laughed. She had no teeth. I ran my tongue over my own to make sure they were still there.

She kept laughing and laughing and reached up like she wanted to take me, but there was no way I was getting into bed with a raisin lady, so I held on to Mom's neck as tight as I could, while simultaneously trying to crawl on top of her head. Mom compromised by sitting down on the bed with me. Great-grandmama just kept giggling, and looking at me, and finally when I was sure Mom wasn't going to stick me in bed with her and leave me there, I relaxed my grip a little and took a good look at my great-grandmother. She stopped laughing, but kept smiling, and I smiled right back at her. And then she started laughing again, and I did too.

We shared a good laugh, and then she died. I kept laughing, even when everyone else got quiet and one of the more hysterical relatives called for the nurse, and then it wasn't so cute that I was still laughing, and I got in trouble, but I couldn't stop. It was just so funny, what she told me with her eyes. I wish I could remember what it was.

5

'Take your seats, please, ladies. We have two items of business this morning,' Mr Mueller gobbles, standing at the front of the class. 'Frank and Cray, please report to the principal's office.'

Cray doesn't look at any of us. He just gets up and walks toward the door, wordlessly taking the hall pass Mr Mueller holds out to him.

Frank makes a big deal out of getting up slowly and stretching, and then leans over to Thea and whispers, 'No worries, babe, right?'

She smiles back at him. 'No worries.'

'Franklin!' Mr Mueller says loudly, interrupting Frank's suave move-in-for-a-kiss moment. 'To the office. Now.'

Frank winks at Pilar and me. We both give him the finger. He leans down to Ben and whispers, 'Next time. I promise.' Which makes Mr Mueller yell at him again. As soon as Frank's out of the room, we all look over at Thea.

'You going to tell us what that's about?'

Thea rearranges her books on her desk, unable to hide her smirk.

'Where were you last night?' MayBe asks in her soft voice. 'My mom thought you were coming home. We set a place for you.'

'Sorry,' Thea says, glancing at MayBe. 'We got caught up.'

'In *what*?' I ask.

'You'll find out,' Thea says, crossing her arms and leaning back in her chair.

'Thea . . .' MayBe looks like she might cry. 'What are you up to?'

Ben listens to all of this without turning around. He keeps his arms crossed in front of him, his legs stretched out, staring straight ahead. I can tell he's pissed.

'New girl!' Pilar whispers. 'Oh my God, she looks like she's in elementary school.'

The new girl has her red hair pulled into two braided pigtails that curl under her earlobes. It's a hairstyle that no one in the eleventh grade has worn for at least seven years, but something about it suits her. With her flowered shirt tucked neatly into her corduroys, there's something carefully sweet about the way she's dressed, right down to the hand-drawn hearts on her sneakers.

The whole class watches as she hands a note to Mr Mueller and stands watching him read it.

'She's nervous,' I hear MayBe whisper next to me. 'Look how pale she is.'

'I don't think she's gotten her boobies yet,' Thea whispers back.

Mr Mueller's glare silences our hushed laughter.

'Class,' Mr Mueller says, standing. 'Our second item of business has just arrived. This is Catherine Ritter, she –'

'You can call me Cate,' the girl says cheerfully, before turning bright red and saying to Mr Mueller, 'Oh, sorry, you go ahead.'

He gives her a flat smile and starts again. 'This is Cate and she comes to our mountain from . . .' He smiles at Cate expectantly.

She looks blankly at him for a second before saying, 'Oh! My turn?' She giggles nervously and says to the class, 'I'm from back east.'

Mr Mueller keeps looking at her, waiting for more.

'Can I sit down now, please?' Cate asks. 'I'm just really nervous,' she whispers to Mr Mueller.

'Oh. Yes, of course,' Mr Mueller says. 'Welcome to Paradise –'

Cate flinches at the indignant chorus of 'Pine

113

Mountain!' and slips into the empty seat next to me.

'That was mortifying,' she whispers.

'You did fine,' I say. 'I'm Dylan.'

'Cate,' she says. 'Nice to meet you.'

She looks closely at me for a second, but before she can say anything else, I say, 'This is my best friend, Pilar,' leaning back so Pilar can give Cate a barely perceptible nod.

'Charmed,' Pilar says flatly.

'And that's MayBe, and that's Thea,' I say, pointing to my friends. 'And that's Ben.' Ben still doesn't turn around, he just nods, still facing ahead.

'Hi!' Thea and MayBe say at the same time. 'So, where are you living?' Thea asks.

'Well, we're staying by the lake in an apartment for now. But we're building a place up on the ridge.'

'Are you in those Lakeview apartments?' Pilar asks.

Cate nods. 'Why?'

'None of us have ever been inside them,' I say quickly, before Pilar can answer.

'Frank's dad's been inside,' Thea says. 'He's the facilities manager there. Says they're all right. Overpriced.'

'They put the best beach on the lake behind gates when they built those apartments,' Pilar says. 'You have to live there to get in now.'

'Oh,' Cate says brightly. 'Well, if we're still there in the summer, you guys should come swimming!'

'Not really the point,' Pilar says.

'But thanks,' I say.

'Yeah, thanks,' MayBe and Thea say together.

Frank and Cray miss the first three periods of school, and by the time they walk down the hall, silent and grinning, having been dropped off back at school by Deputy Pesquera, the whole school knows they're the ones who put Super Glue in the locks of the tractors and construction office trailers in the Willows development by the lake.

The boys, Ben included – looking less pissed off than he was this morning – stop by our lunch table long enough for Frank to play tonsil hockey with Thea, and for Cray to lean over and whisper in my ear, 'Pesquera says hello.' I flinch away from him, pretending I didn't hear. He follows Ben and Frank to their lunch table, turning once to look back at me.

'There she is!'

'Don't point at her!' MayBe squeals, grabbing Thea's arm to keep her from pointing at Cate, who's working her way through the lunch line.

'What?' Thea asks, pointing with her other hand.

115

'You're such a brat,' MayBe says, pinning Thea's hands by sitting in her lap, before bucking right back out of it. 'No pinching!'

'Dylan, you're nice to strangers. You call her over here,' Thea says.

I look at Pilar.

'You don't need my permission,' she says. 'Call that little tweety bird right over.'

'Call her over here!' Thea says.

'*Do* it,' MayBe says.

'OK,' I say, standing. 'I'll do it.'

I start to walk toward the lunch line and see Cate coming straight at us. I turn to the table and whisper, 'She's coming over!'

'Sit!' MayBe says, pulling down on my arm. 'Act natural.'

I sit, and when Cate comes walking over, we're all smiling at her like idiots. Even Pilar's smirk is only half wicked. She cocks her head to the side. 'You guys don't have new kids very often, do you?'

The long silence that follows is broken by MayBe crowing, 'Like, never! You're the first new girl in three years! Will you sit with us? I promise we're not evil or anything.' She pats the empty seat next to her and says solemnly, 'We're good people.'

'Do you remember our names?' Thea asks as Cate sits down.

'Um, I think so,' Cate says, pointing at each of us in turn, 'You're Thea, then Dylan, Pilar, and MayBe, right? MayBe – is that short for something?'

'No,' MayBe says quickly, half-burying her head in the cotton tote bag she brought her lunch in. She starts pulling things out, and I see that there's enough for Thea, too.

'Yes, it is,' Thea says. 'MayBe, tell her what your name is short for.'

'Yeah, MayBe,' I say, 'tell her what it stands for.'

'Wait,' Cate says, her voice getting louder. 'Wait a *minute*. I know you!'

She points to MayBe and shouts, 'MoonBaby Honeysuckle Riverwater!'

'Holy crap!' Pilar says, laughing. 'How did she know that?'

'I love your shampoo!' Cate squeals, sticking her head right under MayBe's nose. 'Here! Smell!'

MayBe sniffs. 'Morning Honeydew?'

'Yes!' Cate says. 'It's my favourite. I can't believe I'm sitting here talking to MoonBaby. You look just like you do on the labels! Except, um, you're not a baby.'

MayBe's mom and dad used to own this organic beauty products company called Open Earth. They started it the summer they were living with just-born MayBe in a teepee on the land they were building their solar-powered dome house on. They started out making Mountain Berry Bath Soap and selling it out in front of Sheboa's grocery and by the snack bar at the town beach, walking the long distance to either place from their teepee, with MayBe curled in a handmade cotton sling strapped to her dad's back. It was her little pie face on the label, above the carefully written words *Made with Love*, and you couldn't tell if that referred to MayBe, or the soap, or both. When fall came and the weather turned, Mrs Sheboa started selling the soaps inside the grocery store, letting all the money from what sold – and whatever else the Sheboas could spare – go into a standing house account so MayBe's parents could buy food. That winter they finished the dome house and started making all different kinds of soap, and the business totally took off. More and more soaps and shampoos, all with MayBe's face on the label, all with cute little stories about her little hippie family and their life on the mountain.

'They sold the company, you know,' Pilar says, the laughter gone from her voice, her studied calmness returned.

'What?' Cate's brow wrinkles for a second.

'My parents sold the company,' MayBe says, with a look at Pilar. 'Five years ago.'

'Your Morning Honeydew is fresh from an industrial park in the flatlands. In Taluga. You probably passed it on your way up the mountain,' Pilar says, patting Cate's hand. 'Sorry.'

'That's so sad!' Cate says. 'I used to make my dad read me the stories on the labels while he gave me a bath. I loved the one about how when you were two, you discovered the recipe for the Blueberry Body Wash by putting blueberries and soy milk in the bathtub and splashing around because you were trying to make a smoothie. I used to pretend I was a part of your family.' Cate blushes and presses her fingers to her lips. 'Oh, sorry, is that weird?'

'I still pretend that!' Thea laughs.

'I can't believe it's not true any more,' Cate says.

'It's not like I told you there's no such thing as Santa,' Pilar says. 'I think you'll get over it.'

Cate just looks at her, biting her lower lip.

'Wait, you *do* know about Santa, don't you?' Pilar says.

I turn to her. 'Professor, stop trying to make the new kid cry.'

'She's fine!' Pilar says, motioning to Cate. 'She can take – Oh, crap, she's crying.'

Cate practically slaps away the fat tear that's rolling down her face. 'I'm not crying,' she says.

'Why would you do that?' MayBe says to Pilar, using the hem of her flannel skirt to dab at the tear on Cate's cheek. 'She probably thought we were normal people for a whole five minutes.'

'I'm fine, really,' Cate says, pulling out of MayBe's reach.

'She's bound to find out sooner or later,' Pilar says drily.

'Would you knock it off?' I say loudly. 'Seriously, Professor, take it down a notch. She knows you're the one with the biting sense of humour. She gets it, all right?'

It takes me a second to realise that all motion at the lunch table has stopped.

'Wow, Dylan,' Thea says, 'you really showed some emotion there.'

'What's that supposed to mean?' I ask.

Thea shrugs. 'It's like the red-hot rage melted your icy exterior.'

'I'm not icy,' I say, actually hurt. 'I'm . . . reserved.' I look to Pilar for help.

'I can't believe you *Professored* me in anger,' she says.

'Well, you're the one who broke the new kid!' I say loudly.

'Oh, gosh, please stop fighting,' Cate pleads.

'Who's fighting?' Pilar asks, looking at Cate as though she's just noticed her sitting there.

'We're not fighting,' I agree. 'We're trying to impress you with our witty banter.'

'Oh,' Cate says, 'but isn't witty banter supposed to be, you know, witty?'

Pilar clutches at her chest and collapses against me. 'You don't think we're funny?'

'But our genius sense of comic timing is all we have!' I yelp.

Thea rolls her eyes and says to Cate, 'I bet you thought, being the new kid, you'd get to be the centre of attention for more than half a second.'

'Yeah, Pilar,' I say, pushing her off me, 'stop hogging the spotlight and pay some attention to the new kid.'

Pilar sighs and stage-whispers, 'Like how?'

'I don't know, ask her a question or something. Show some interest.'

'Fine,' Pilar says, turning quickly toward Cate. 'Would you rather be eaten alive by rats or pushed out of a plane without a parachute?'

Cate chooses no parachute, since then she would at least experience what it's like to fly before she dies. Thanks to Pilar, we also find out that Cate would rather eat live worms than live termites, would eat her own big toe if it was the only way to avoid starvation, and would rather have the runs than be throwing up. She's a good sport about the whole thing, making us laugh with her questions like, 'Could I add some slug guts to the worms before I eat them?'

Eventually Pilar pauses long enough for Thea and MayBe to ask some questions too, except theirs are more along the lines of where are you from? ('Massachusetts'), do you have brothers and sisters? ('no, just lots of cousins'), did you have a boyfriend back home? ('we broke up before I moved'), and can Thea please, please do your hair because you've got such a cute face and those double braids do nothing for you? ('I know it looks dumb. It's just the way my dad's done my hair on the first day of school for years and years. It's a tradition').

'Um, Dylan?' Cate's standing next to my locker, holding her books close to her chest. 'I think I'm on your bus today.'

'Actually, you can take any bus. They all pass through the village. That's where your place is, right? That gated

122

community right outside the village? By the Willows?'

She nods a long time before she can find her voice. 'Um, yes, but I'm actually not going home. My dad's with the surveyors up on the back of the land we're building on. That lady, Fran, in the front office said it was up at the dead end by your house. She said I could take the bus to the dead end at the top of your road. That's where my dad is. I'm supposed to meet him there.'

She looks like she might throw up. God, I was such an ass to her yesterday.

'Oh, OK,' I say, smiling. 'It's bus number three. Meet me here after last class; we'll go together.'

'Cool. See you then,' she says, walking off to class.

'See you.'

'It's like an after-school special on how to make new friends,' Pilar says behind me. I turn around. 'You guys are like, what, BFFs now?' she asks.

'Yes, Pilar, she and I are Best Friends Forever because my *twelve years* of friendship with you means nothing to me.'

Pilar studies the end of her braid.

'Pilar, you goober, I'm joking.'

It takes me a second to realise that she's not walking with me. I take three steps backward till I'm standing next to her.

'It's just been a while, you know?' she says. 'Since we've had anyone new. Tell her that I'm not, like, an ogre or something. Tell her it's not on purpose. I just get mean when I get nervous.' Pilar groans. 'She's just so darn cherubic, I feel like I'm going to sully her with my . . . What'd you call it? Biting sense of humour.'

'I think as long as you don't bite her for real, you'll be OK.'

'So you've lived up here your whole life?' Cate asks, as the bus pulls out of the driveway and on to Lakeshore Drive. We're sitting near the back.

'Yep,' I say proudly. 'I was one of the first babies born in the new hospital.'

'Wait. I thought the new hospital wasn't built yet. At least that's what it said in the handy-dandy Paradise Mountain welcome brochure.'

I groan. 'It's not Paradise Mountain yet.'

She smiles at me. 'You still call it Pine Mountain! I love that. I will too, then. So, what about the hospital?'

'They're building a *new* new one. I guess it's good. It'll be bigger, have more services and a whole section for old people who can't live at home. So I guess I mean I was one of the first born at the old hospital,' I say.

I give Cate a history lesson in the two minutes it takes to drive through the village.

'So the Sheboas just up and moved?'

'Sort of. They moved over to Baker's Creek, on the other side of the mountain. There's, like, nothing over there, but they opened a grocery store anyway. People say Baker's is like what this side used to be before all the development.'

'What were you doing there yesterday?' Cate asks when we pass by the police station.

'Picking something up for my mom,' I say quickly. 'What about you?'

'Same thing. A dog licence application for our mutt, Newman. He farts a lot, but I let him sleep in bed with me anyway.'

The bus slows and turns on to my road.

'You live with your mom and dad?' she asks.

'My mom. My dad's not around.'

'Neither's my mom,' she says. 'She's been getting her rest for the past ten years.'

I have no idea what to say to this, so I stutter something like, 'Oh m-my God.'

'Oh, she's not dead!' Cate says quickly. 'She's in the hospital. And your dad?'

'Just not around.'

'Gottcha. I don't like to talk about my mom, either. Are there any actual houses up here?' she says, looking out the window at the dense groves of trees covering both sides of the road.

'Just two. That's Ben's house,' I say, pointing to the end of Ben's driveway peeking out through the trees. 'Mine's right up here.'

'And the dead end?'

'Is just a little further up. Dottie can drop you off. Or,' I say, my stomach jumping, 'do you want to come in for a snack before you go see your dad? I can walk you up after, if you want.'

'I would love to!'

Before we're even through the front door Cate announces right off that she loves my house.

'It's adorable,' she says, standing in the middle of our cramped living room.

'It's tiny,' I answer, turning on the light. It's getting dark. Winter dark, but no winter snow. 'It was a logger's cabin. My parents added stuff – the kitchen and the two bedrooms upstairs, and the porch and the bathrooms, but it's mostly the same size as when they bought it.'

'I love that, though!' Cate says. 'It's like you have everything you need right here.' I follow her gaze to the woodstove in the fireplace, to the old wooden-legged couch that faces it, and the faded rugs covering the wide-pine floors. She bursts out laughing when she sees the flat-screen TV we have mounted above the fireplace.

'Come see the kitchen,' I say. 'We have a microwave, too.'

'You're funny,' she says, before announcing that she loves our cracked oak table, the old-fashioned white stove my mom rescued from the dump, and the last of the fall flowers that are sticking out of a dented metal pitcher in the kitchen.

We're standing on the foggy back deck, its triangle tip jutting out over the tops of the trees barely visible in the mist, when it starts to rain again.

'You should call your dad and see if you can just stay here till he's done up there,' I say when we're back inside.

Cate calls her dad, and it turns out he's giving up because of the rain. He agrees to come back and pick her up later on. We hear him beep his horn when he drives by.

'Don't worry,' she says, 'it's still going to be just you and Ben on this road. Our driveway is going to be clear on the other side of the ridge. But maybe we can build a trail

127

from my house to yours! It would run just a mile or so; we could meet up in the middle for camp-outs!'

I tell her I think it's a really good idea, and make us some hot chocolate and microwave brownies.

It's Cate's idea for me to show her pictures of everyone from when we were kids. We sit on the rug in front of the woodstove, which I took the liberty of lighting because our house is absolutely freezing, even in the early days of this no-snow winter. We lean against the couch, a pile of photo albums in front of us. I reach for the album labelled *First Grade*, but Cate touches my hand and says, 'Wait. Start with kindergarten.' She pulls the heavy green album labelled *Kindergarten* off the bookshelf next to the fireplace where I'd left it, and hands it to me.

'OK.' I take the book and open it to the first page. Our class picture.

'Is that you?' she asks right away, pointing to where I sat in the front row.

I nod. 'And there's Pilar and MayBe and Thea.'

'You guys are so cute!' she crows, taking the album into her lap and bending over it to look more closely. 'OK, who is everyone else?'

I run my fingers across the rows, telling her people's

names and whether or not they still live on the mountain. When I get to Clarence I just say his name, and move on to Frank, who sat next to him.

'Wait, what's his story?' Cate asks.

'Who, Frank?' I ask, shrugging. 'He's all right. He used to eat all the paste during craft time.'

'Gross, but no, the kid next to Frank. You said his name *was* Clarence?'

I look at her.

'You said that, right?' she says quickly. 'His name is Clarence?'

'You were right the first time,' I answer. '*Was*. His name *was* Clarence.'

'You mean he moved away?'

'Nobody's told you about this?'

'About what? You're freaking me out a little, here,' she says, laughing nervously.

I wish Pilar were here. She'd know how to handle this. She'd just say it, matter-of-factly. 'Clarence was killed, when we were in kindergarten.'

Cate watches me as I say it, and colour drains out of her face. 'Who would do something like that?' she asks.

'They don't know. They never caught the guy who did it.'

'Oh my God,' she moans, 'that's so scary. So, he's still out there?'

'It depends who you ask,' I say, leaning over to look at the photos. 'Deputy Pesquera thinks the Drifter – that's what the kids call the guy who killed Clarence – she thinks he just drifted right off the mountain. Some people think he's still up here, though, waiting.'

'What do you think?'

'I think he's long gone,' I say, with more confidence than I feel.

'Did Clarence always wear his glasses?' she asks quietly, leaning so close her nose is almost touching the photograph.

I nod.

She looks at me with wet eyes and sniffs. 'Why does that make it even sadder?' She laughs a little, shaking her head. 'Little kid-size plastic glasses. Jesus.'

'They were green,' I say, 'and in the sun they would make his cheeks green too.'

'He looks like a frog,' she says, smiling.

'We called him Frogger,' I answer.

'Well,' she says, carefully closing the album. 'That's just about the saddest thing I've ever heard in my entire life.'

'Sorry,' I say.

'You must have been really scared when it happened. Do you remember it?'

I shrug. 'Yeah, but . . . it's not something we talk about up here. I think people would just rather forget it ever happened.'

'But you don't forget, right? You can't ever forget something like that. Especially because this year would be . . . what? The eleventh anniversary?'

'I guess so. The first week of December.'

'What's this?' Cate asks, opening to the back of the album.

'We had these made,' I say, pulling out a carefully folded T-shirt that's slipped against the back cover, 'for the one-year memorial.' The T-shirt is green, Clarence's favourite colour. On it is the school picture of Clarence, and written underneath is *We Miss Our Friend.*

'Were you ever this small?' Cate asks, holding up the tiny shirt.

I take it back from her and re-fold it.

'Want to see first grade?' I ask, opening another album.

'Sure, but can I use your bathroom first?'

'Yep. It's at the top of the stairs.'

I re-shelve the kindergarten book while Cate's upstairs. I hear a flush and then, 'Your room's so cute!'

I'm kind of annoyed. My room's a total wreck, and I wasn't really expecting anyone but my mom to see my collection of underwear spanning the floor. I stand at the bottom of the stairs and look up as the light from my bedroom spills into the upstairs hallway.

'Thanks,' I say, starting up the stairs. 'Are you coming back down?'

She pokes her head around the corner. 'I have stars on my ceiling too!'

She goes back into my room, and when I get to the top of the stairs and turn to follow her, I see her standing by my bureau, holding a small photograph. I freeze. She holds the photograph up to me.

'This is that little girl from the news, right? The one who got killed in the desert. Why do you have this?'

I step quickly forward and grab Tessa's photograph away from her and stuff it into my pocket, crumpling it as I do.

'Did you know her?' Cate asks. 'Did you know that little girl?'

'No,' I answer.

'Then why . . .' Cate stops talking, her face pales. 'I don't understand. Why do you have her picture?'

I am calmer than I thought I would be. I always

pictured that this moment would happen with Pilar, and that it would be deafening in its noise. Confessing, yelling, crying, questioning. Sometimes I think we would just cling to each other after, and she would tell me she forgave me for never telling her, and that nothing in our friendship would change. Most of the time, though, I picture her walking away from me, and never looking back.

This is the moment, but it's the wrong moment. I know that I can stop it. I know that I can think of an excuse that will explain the bent photograph in my pocket. I know that I can make this better. I don't, though, because suddenly I know that if I don't tell someone, if I don't say this out loud, I am going to die.

'You can't tell anyone,' I say, finally.

'Tell anyone what?'

'What I'm about to tell you.'

'OK.'

'The first time it happened was with Clarence . . .'

It doesn't feel as good as I thought it would. I don't feel any relief, I feel only sick. Cate is sitting on the braided rug, leaning against my bed. I am across from her, sitting against my bureau. I look at the clock on the nightstand. She's been quiet for three minutes.

'Cate?'

She looks at me, almost helplessly. 'And you never see them alive?' she asks. Again.

I shake my head. 'I only see them after it's happened.'

She goes silent again. 'What *good* is that?' she asks, the bite in her voice making me reel back. 'I'm sorry,' she says. 'This is all just too messed up.'

'I know,' I say.

'How many times?' she asks. 'How many times have you . . . seen something.'

'Maybe eight,' I say. 'Not once a year, but pretty close.'

'And all those kids, was it ever the Drifter that did it?' It's so weird, hearing a stranger use his name.

'Never.'

'I think,' she says, getting unsteadily to her feet, 'I'm going to wait outside for my dad.'

'Are you OK?' I ask, standing.

She shakes her head. 'Yes. No.' She shrugs and almost laughs. 'I don't know. Is this what you tell all the new kids?' She walks toward the bedroom door, and I step in front of her.

'Nobody else knows about this, Cate. Just my mom and Deputy Pesquera and Sheriff Dean. They can't know that I told you. I wasn't supposed to tell anyone.'

We both jump when my mom opens the front door downstairs.

'It got cold!' Mom says, and I hear her stamping the rain off her feet on to the doormat. 'Please remember,' she calls up the stairs, 'to turn the porch light on so your poor mother doesn't trip and break her neck.'

Cate and I haven't moved.

'I won't tell,' Cate finally says. 'Can I please go now?'

'Oh,' I say, realising I'm still blocking her path, and I move out of her way. 'Yeah.'

'And who's this?' Mom asks when Cate starts down the steps.

'I'm Cate,' she says, and I wonder if my mom can hear her forced brightness. 'I just started at the high school today.'

'Nice to meet you, Cate,' Mom says, shaking Cate's outstretched hand. Cate moves past her down the stairs.

'My dad's coming to pick me up,' she says. 'I'm just going to wait outside.'

'Nonsense,' Mom says, with a disapproving look at me where I'm sitting at the top of the steps. 'It's freezing out. You can stay in until he comes.'

Outside, a car horn beeps.

'That's him,' Cate says to my mom, before looking

up at me. 'I'll see you tomorrow, Dylan. Thanks for having me over.'

'Let me come outside and say hello,' Mom says, putting on her coat again.

'Oh, gosh, maybe next time,' Cate says quickly, grabbing her coat and book bag. 'He's in a really big rush tonight. It was nice meeting you! Oh, sorry,' she says, waiting till my mom moves out of the way before she opens up the door.

'You too,' Mom says, holding the door open so Cate can't close it. I walk downstairs and see Mom step on to the front porch and wave to Cate's dad.

'Well, she's just cute as a button,' Mom says, coming back inside. 'She just started today?'

'Mm-hm. She's from back east.' I start putting the photo albums back on the bookshelf.

'You guys were looking at pictures?' Mom asks.

I don't answer, just finish putting away the books.

'Did you tell her about Clarence?' she asks, eyeing the kindergarten book.

I shrug. 'I mentioned it.'

'And that's all you mentioned?' she asks sharply.

I glare at her. 'Yes, that's all I mentioned.'

'Good,' she says, smiling. 'You still look tired. I want

you in bed early tonight. I'm going to get changed.'

The phone rings when Mom is halfway upstairs. 'I'll get it,' she says. I hear her saying, 'Hello, Ruby. No, she has homework to do,' before she closes the door to her bedroom.

I open up the kindergarten photo album again. I lift the clear plastic sheet covering the photographs, and unpeel Clarence's wallet-size image from the page. Then I put the album back on the shelf.

Upstairs, I close my bedroom door and sit on the braided rug, leaning against my bed, right where Cate sat not even an hour ago. Like re-enacting a crime, I think. I reach over to my nightstand and pull a small white envelope from the drawer.

The seven photographs are slippery in my fingers. I stack them together, like playing cards.

The first picture was cut out of a larger group photo-graph. The very top of the girl Angela's head is covered by someone's hairy and suntanned arm. Her dad's, I think. They are at a summertime party, a picnic by a lake. Angela's cheeks are sunburned, and she's laughing like she's being tickled. It was so quick with Angela, I wasn't sure at first I'd even really had a vision. But it kept coming, like a quick pulse that I had to work to slow down until I could see what was happening. It helped her parents to know that it was quick for her, that she didn't understand what was happening, that she didn't even have the chance to be afraid.

The memories of the kids in the next two pictures always run together for me, because their deaths happened only months apart, and because the two kids looked sort of alike. What happened to them couldn't have been more different, though. With Noah, the first one, I kept smelling something burning. I was eleven and just barely allowed to boil my own water for hot chocolate, so that whole Saturday I kept checking the stove, thinking maybe that I'd left a burner on that morning. Mom finally grabbed me, literally grabbed my arm on my bazillionth trip to the stove, and asked me what was going on. She didn't smell anything burning, she assured me. But the burning smell was starting to drive me crazy. I smelled it even when I held my nose closed. It wasn't till that night that I saw him. By that time, he didn't look like he did in his picture. He didn't look like anything any more. Fiona happened just a few months later, and she looked just like herself, except lying crooked at the bottom of a well her parents didn't even know was in their backyard.

Morgan. She had fat earlobes that she wore heart

earrings in; she had a mole on her left cheek, and eyebrows that seemed too thick for a five-year-old. *Like me*, I remember thinking. They found her at the neighbour's house, once they figured out I was describing what Morgan's house looked like from his bedroom window.

Then came Tim. *Not Timmy*, I remember his mom saying on the news, *Tim*. I don't like to think about what happened to him. I saw too much red.

The next picture is of Wesley and his neatly parted hair. When it happened I was nine, he was six. In the picture he has a toothy, wide-mouthed smile and a pudgy little face. He was the one I could feel drowning as I sat with my mom and dad in church one Sunday. My dad started whacking me on the back, because I was turning blue while the pastor was announcing the date for that year's summer social. Mom carried me into the bathroom, sitting me on the sink and rubbing my arms up and down until I was breathing again. They said what happened to Wesley wasn't exactly murder, but I think it was. I think his sister knew she held him under for just a little too long.

My dad found my mom in the church bathroom, when she was trying to get me to breath again. He wanted to call for an ambulance, but she wouldn't let him. She said, *She's OK, Marty, she'll be OK*. I remember my dad looking at me in a way he never had before. I was saying, *The boy can't breathe. Let him out of the water, Mommy, he can't breathe.* I could see my own distorted reflection in the metal paper-towel holder, my chin stretched out, my eyes black holes. I still think that's what he saw. I still think that maybe that's what I really look like. A monster. He said, *She has it, doesn't she?* And then, three days later, he was gone.

The last picture is the same picture of Clarence that I just took from the photo album. The one from the envelope is more faded, but the one from the album is curved from being peeled off the adhesive. I place one of the Clarence pictures on one knee, and the picture of Tessa, smoothed out, on the other. You can't tell, from looking at the pictures, that they are linked forever now. I think, *I am linked to them too.* My stomach clenches when I think of the fourth figure, linked to all of us, no matter how hard I may try to sever the invisible tendon tying us all together.

That night, when I dream of the desert, I try again and again to turn around, finding myself either facing in the same direction or unable to move at all. The footsteps get closer and closer, but there is never a cold hand on my shoulder or a hard shove sending me into the hole. The fear is too much. *Wake up, wake up, wake up.* I do.

6

Mom bangs on the bathroom door the next morning, telling me that Cate is waiting for me outside. I take an oversize Band-Aid from the medicine cabinet and carefully place the photographs of Tessa and Clarence in its centre. Then I press the Band-Aid over my heart.

'Did you know she was riding the bus with you this morning?' Mom asks when I get downstairs.

'Yeah,' I lie. 'Didn't I tell you?'

'No,' she says firmly.

I get out the front door as quickly as I can.

'Hi,' Cate says, turning to look at me from where she sits on our front steps.

'Hi,' I answer, closing the front door behind me.

'My dad had to come back up here this morning. He said I should ride the bus with you.' Cate stands up and walks down the steps. She waits for me at the bottom.

We walk in silence to the bottom of the driveway,

where we stand stomping our feet against the cold. I wish it would just snow already.

'I'm sorry about last night,' she says.

'Why would you be sorry?' I ask. 'I'm the one who should be sorry. I shouldn't have laid all that on you.'

She shrugs. 'It must have felt good to finally tell someone.'

I snort. 'Not really. It actually felt pretty rotten.'

'Maybe at first,' she says, 'but I bet you felt better afterward.'

'I guess I did,' I say, 'but I shouldn't have even told you in the first place.'

'But you did tell me,' she says quickly. 'And sorry, sister,' she laughs, 'but you can't get that cat back in the bag.'

I wave to Dottie as she passes by us toward the dead end. 'Nope. I guess I can't.'

She smiles at me. 'You know, a secret is only half as heavy if you have someone to carry it with you.'

I look at her. All of the darkness that clouded her face last night is gone. There is only a cautious smile left, and I have this almost giddy feeling, the same sort of slipping, falling feeling that I get before a vision, but this time I'm the one deciding to take the jump. 'Wow, Cate. That was a really sweet thing to say.'

'I know!' she crows. 'I thought of it last night! I felt so
bad for freaking out at you, and I thought about how hard
it must have been for you to tell me, and how I told you
about my mom being in the nuthouse, which, by the way,
nobody knows about, and how I felt better as soon as I told
you. So there. We both know each other's biggest secret.
Cool, right?'

'Right,' I say, realising it's true.

'And I can ask you about your secret and you can ask
me about mine.'

'OK.'

She keeps on smiling and nodding at me.

'Do you *want* to ask me something?' I finally ask her.

'Yes! I have, like, a million and one questions.'

'Maybe you can start with just one,' I say.

'Oh, come on. *Just one?*'

'Yep,' I say, enjoying this. 'Just one.'

'How about,' she says, her eyes widening with an idea,
'one *every day*. On the way to school – my dad can drop me
off every morning. You can ask me one and I can ask you
one. And we *have* to answer. That's the rule.'

'OK,' I say, glancing up the street. 'You have twenty
seconds before Dottie gets back down here.'

'OK,' she says, narrowing her eyes and screwing up her

143

mouth like she's thinking really hard. 'When was the first time you had a vision?'

My hand flutters automatically to my chest, touching my sweatshirt in the place where the Band-Aid lies beneath. I laugh. 'That was a total waste of a question! I told you last night. When I was five, in kindergarten.'

'That was the first time?'

'Yep.'

'What was the time after that?'

'Too late!' I say. 'You had your one question already.'

'Oh, man!' Cate says, stamping her foot. 'You're right. OK, your turn.'

We step back from the driveway so Dottie can pull up. I wait till we're settled on the bus to ask.

'How old were you when your mom went into the hospital?'

'Five years old,' Cate says. 'Weird, our questions both had the same answers! What do you think that means?'

'Most likely that you're a psychic.'

Her eyes widen. 'Really?'

'No,' I laugh.

The bus stops in front of Ben's house, and this time he gets on with his brothers, JJ and Tye. I wonder if he and Frank had it out or something.

'What's up?' he mumbles as he passes us on his way to the back of the bus.

'Morning!' Cate says.

'Neighbour,' I say.

'"Neighbour." That's cute,' Cate says. 'Do you guys always call each other that?'

'I guess,' I say, still wondering why Ben looks so glum.

'This school is the best,' Cate says, laughing.

'Where were you?' I ask, after finally finding Pilar by spotting her black high-tops under a bathroom stall door. There's a flush, and she comes out of the stall.

'Hello to you, too.' Pilar yawns and turns on the faucet.

I lean against the mirror by the sink so I can face her. 'You weren't in homeroom. Listen . . .'

'I overslept. Listen to what?'

'That girl, Cate, came to my house this morning, and we rode the bus to school together,' I rush out.

'And?'

'And I think she's really lonely and she's going to sit with us for lunch again.'

'Oh, cool.' She looks at me. 'Anything else?'

'Nope. That's all.'

Pilar washes her hands in silence before turning to

me. 'So you came in here to warn me? You think I was going to make her cry again? I didn't do it on purpose, you know.'

She actually sounds defensive.

'Don't be a goober!' I say, poking her playfully in the arm. 'I just thought you'd want to know.'

'Well, thanks for telling me.'

'So, she's sitting with us at lunch.'

Pilar turns to me. 'I heard you the first time.'

'I know,' I say. 'I just . . .'

'You want me to be nice to her?'

'Well, yeah.'

'Fine. She's not coming this afternoon, is she? To Thea's?'

I'd actually been planning on inviting her, but – 'No, of course not. It's just us four.'

'Good,' Pilar says, hip checking me out of her way.

Pilar's taken her new pledge to be supernice to Cate really seriously. She insists on carrying Cate's tray through the lunch line, and pointing out the food she least suspects to be laced with mouse turds. 'You really should just brown-bag it,' Pilar says when they get back to our lunch table.

'Or,' MayBe says with a smile, 'you could use this.' She

pulls a folded canvas bag out of her backpack and hands it to Cate. 'I found it in the crawl space under our house. Thought maybe you'd like it.'

'I love it!' Cate shouts, holding the bag out for us to see. The Open Earth logo is a circle with a baby picture of MayBe right in the middle. '*Made with Love*,' Cate reads aloud. 'Thank you! I really, really love it.' She hugs MayBe.

'You should have seen them all last night,' Thea says. 'MayBe's mom and dad pulling out all of the old stuff from the company. All these notebooks with handwritten soap recipes, and rough drafts of the stories that ended up on the labels. It was, like, the cutest thing I've ever seen.'

'What do your parents do now?' Cate asks.

'They're Internet investment bankers,' MayBe says. 'They sort of lost their taste for organic products.'

'Why?'

I look at MayBe. It's the same question she asked her parents again and again when they sold Open Earth. She cried and cried and begged them not to sell it.

'They said they stopped believing that products made with love could really change the world. And of course they wanted to make enough money to put surveillance cameras up around our property and to put an alarm system in.' Thea touches MayBe's arm and MayBe stops talking. She looks at Cate. 'We had a tragedy up here when we were in kindergarten. It changed things.'

'She knows,' I say, holding my breath beneath the heavy stares of my friends, until Pilar shrugs and says, 'So, she knows, then.'

There is a long, quiet moment and then Cate says, 'I'm really sorry about what happened on your mountain. That must have been really terrible for all of you.'

Thea and Pilar shrug, and MayBe says softly, 'Thanks, Cate.'

I don't say anything; I just wait to see what will happen.

'But why?' Cate asks. 'Why couldn't they catch him? I mean, nobody had any idea who did it?'

'Oh, everyone had ideas about who did it,' Pilar says darkly.

'God, that's right!' I say, remembering. 'People thought it was Sheriff Dean for a while.'

'Or Mr Sheboa,' Thea says. 'People suspected Fran's husband, too.'

'People suspected everyone's husband,' MayBe says, 'and my dad.'

'And *my* dad,' Pilar says.

'Every man on this mountain was a suspect,' MayBe says. 'It was awful. We weren't allowed to go to each other's houses, we weren't allowed to play outside. . . .'

'But none of them was the Drifter?' Cate asks.

'Nope. They had evidence. And they tested it against every single man up here, and none of them matched.'

'That's when they came up with their Drifter theory.'

'It wasn't just that, though. It was that they found his camp.'

'That could have been anybody's camp. There's lots of people camped out in these woods –'

'So he's still out there?' Cate asks, interrupting.

Thea shrugs. 'I bet he's long gone.'

'Why?' Cate asks.

'Because it's been almost eleven years, and he hasn't come back yet, so . . .'

'So what?' Pilar asks.

'*So*, he's not up here any more, that's what!' Thea says loudly.

'But he could be in the desert,' Pilar says. 'It could have been him that got that little girl in the desert.'

'And it could have been the Easter Bunny, too!' Thea says loudly. 'You guys are depressing me. I'm going to the library.'

MayBe leaves with her, and then Pilar, who says she has a headache, goes to lie down in the nurse's office,

149

saying she doesn't need me to go with her, before I can even offer.

Cate looks at me across the empty table. 'I guess we know how to clear a room.'

'Guess so,' I say absently, wondering when Sheriff Dean is going to make the announcement about the metal shavings. I wonder what will change when he does. Sometimes I think people up here are as strong as the mountain we live on, and sometimes I think the littlest thing could make us all crumble down into the flatlands.

'What'd you guys do for fun when you were little?'

'What?'

'Like, for fun. What'd you do?'

I shrug. 'I don't know. Normal stuff. Played in the woods, went to the Niner for birthday parties, made bird feeders out of pine cones and peanut butter . . .'

'What's the Niner?'

'The Miner Forty-Niner. You pass it on your way up the mountain; it's that restaurant that looks like it's about to fall over the edge.'

'The one with the giant horseshoe hanging over the door? Please,' Cate says, her hands gripping the table, 'tell me it's a restaurant with a gold rush theme.'

I laugh. 'Matter of fact . . .'

'Yes!' she squeals. 'Do you want to go this weekend? We can invite MayBe and Thea and Pilar, too.'

'That place is crawling with flatlanders now,' I groan. But the way Cate is holding her breath makes me say, 'But yeah, let's go this weekend. It'll be fun.'

Cate wiggles in her seat. 'So awesome.'

'She could have come with us!' MayBe says, as we wave out the bus window to Cate. 'Dylan, why didn't you invite her?'

'Oh, come on,' Pilar says, 'she's lived up here for a minute and a half. We don't need to adopt her.'

'So that's why!' Thea says, poking Pilar in the side. 'You're jealous of freckle face.'

'Shove it,' Pilar says, putting her backpack between her and Thea. 'I'm not jealous. I just wanted it to be us four today. Is that so wrong?'

'*Is that so wrong?*' Thea laughs.

'It's sort of sweet, actually,' MayBe says, smiling at Pilar. 'You like us!'

The plan is to meet up with Thea's mom in the centre of the village before going back to Thea's so she can cut my hair. We go to the pharmacy first, so Thea can pick up some supplies for her mom, which for some reason Thea seems really annoyed about. Pilar and I sit on the bench outside of Mountain Candy, the overhang sheltering us from the rain, and let MayBe go into the pharmacy with the fuming Thea.

'The Niner? What is she, a six-year-old?' Pilar's not exactly thrilled with Cate's Miner Forty-Niner plan. She scowls at me, and then scowls at the Christmas-light-wrapped evergreen trees that now bookend the bench we're sitting on, along with the other benches in the village and every other non-moving object. Even though it's only four o'clock, it's already dark enough for the lights to be turned on. 'This place looks like Rudolph threw up on it.'

'Oh, come on, Professor, it's a winter wonderland,' I say, offering her the bag of Sour Patch Kids we just bought. 'You know you love it.'

'It's not even Thanksgiving yet!'

'Thems the rules,' I say, sucking on a candy. Last year, in order to 'extend the holiday buying season', the Village Business Association voted to put the holiday decorations up two weeks before Thanksgiving, instead of waiting till the day after, like they usually did.

I love the way it looks, and I think Pilar does too. Even the headlights and tail lights on the cars, shining against the rain-wet pavement, give me a cosy feeling.

Pilar rifles through the candy bag and pulls out a bunch in her hand. I take the green ones from her, my favourites, and leave her the rest. She pops them all into her mouth at once.

'You'll come, though, right? To the Niner tomorrow?'

Pilar pulls another Sour Patch Kid out of the bag and holds it between her teeth and says, 'Whshe ish matter sho you.'

'Because it'll be fun,' I say. 'That's a green one.'

Pilar spits out the green Sour Patch Kid. 'Fine. I'll go. But if she wears some creepy six-year-old party dress, I'm vacating the premises.'

Thea and MayBe come out of the pharmacy and I tell them about the Niner plan.

'Sweet. That place has good curly fries,' Thea says.

We huddle under the overhang for a few minutes more, delaying the moment when we have to run across the street in the rain to where Thea's mom is shopping at Old Sheboa's, which is what everyone's decided to call the grocery store.

'I wish it'd just snow already,' MayBe sighs.

'*First snow's coming and he's coming back,*' Thea says, pulling her hood up over her head. It takes her a second to realise we're all looking at her. 'What? We always say that.'

153

It's true; we've been saying that before the first snow for years. It has sort of lost its meaning.

Thea snorts. 'What? All of a sudden we realise how creepy that stupid song is?'

'It *is* kind of creepy,' MayBe says, looking at me.

'I hate that song,' Pilar says. Why's she looking at me too?

'Me too,' I say. Thea snorts again, but doesn't say anything.

We wait for the traffic going through town to slow, and then we run across the street, our feet slapping wetly against the asphalt. In the grocery store we find Thea's mom in the fruit department, filling a bag with green apples.

'You girls get what you needed?' she asks.

'Yes, we got what *you* needed,' Thea says, and the vein of darkness when she speaks pushes MayBe, Pilar, and me to start sampling imported cherries on the other end of the aisle.

MayBe watches Thea and her mom start to argue, a cherry bulging out her cheek as she chews. 'You know that I love it when Thea stays with me,' she says, quietly. 'I just wish she and her mom could get along.'

Pilar spits a cherry pit to the floor and kicks it under

154

the strawberry display. 'They'll be fine,' she says. 'My mom and I barely talk any more, and we actually get along better now than before.'

'You didn't tell me that!' I say.

She shrugs. 'We've been fighting since that night you came over to babysit.'

'Why?'

'Because she's crazy, that's why,' Pilar says sharply.

'Well, yeah, Pilar, all moms act crazy. It's, like, their favourite hobby,' I say earnestly. 'You can't just stop talking to her.'

'Why does this matter to you?' Pilar asks, almost hitting my sneaker with a cherry pit.

'It doesn't,' I say, stuffing a few cherries into my mouth to cover the waver in my voice. 'I just . . . you didn't tell me.'

'I don't *have* to tell you everything,' Pilar says, scowling at me.

'Yes, you *do*!' I shout, spitting out a glob of cherries. Pilar's scowl flicks up at the edges, and even this tiniest hint of a smile makes me smile too. 'It's totally in the best friend rule book. You, Professor,' I say, pointing at her, 'are breaking the rules.'

As soon as I say it, I feel like the linoleum floor is

going to open up and swallow me whole for being such a hypocrite.

'You're one to talk!' Pilar says. 'I saw you and Cate on the bus, whispering in each other's ears.'

I shrug and force a laugh. 'That's just Cate. She thinks everything's worth whispering in your ear.'

'Maybe she likes how your ear smells,' MayBe says absently, watching as Thea and her mom hug. 'They made up. Let's go.'

Pilar leans in, sniffs my ear, and then flicks it. 'Smells like wax.'

Thea cuts my hair while her mom stands behind her and murmurs directions. Three salon chairs are set up in a row on what we remember as Thea's screened-in porch. Her dad enclosed it and installed all the salon stuff when we were in second grade. The best part about coming to Thea's mom for a haircut is that you usually end up sitting at the kitchen table eating cookies with Thea while her mom and your mom drink tea and gab. That's exactly where MayBe and Pilar are now, raiding the cookie cabinet.

They come back into the salon and sit together on the swirly chair next to mine and take turns reaching over to feed Oreo cookies to me and Thea. It works fine until Thea laughs and spits Oreos into my hair.

'Sweatshirt off, please,' Thea says. 'I think I got some on your neck.'

I take my sweatshirt off, forgetting the large Band-Aid taped across my chest under my T-shirt, until I'm leaning back in the chair, my head in the sink.

'You get a tattoo?' Thea asks.

'Who got a tattoo?'

In a second I'm looking up through soapy eyes at Thea, MayBe, Pilar, and even Thea's mom, all looking down at my chest.

'No,' I say. 'It was a . . . mole. I got it removed at the doctor.'

'Gross,' Pilar says.

'Did you keep it?' MayBe asks. 'You could bury it in your yard or something.'

'Um, no. The doctor kept it.'

My hair, after the haircut and second wash, looks almost the same as when I came in, just a little shorter. It's fine with me; I'm sort of attached to the porcupine look. I pay Thea with a stack of Oreos from the cookie cabinet.

We all pile into the backseat of Thea's mom's car for the ride home. The rain pelts the car's roof, and we all sing along to the radio. Thea and her mom have the same husky voice, one that disappears almost completely on the high notes, leaving just a tiny thread of sound that lets you know they're hitting that note straight on.

We're little kids again – eight-year-olds on the way down the hill to the shopping mall in the flatlands. We're all kneecaps and dirty earlobes and friendship pins and Kool-Aid breath.

'Oh, man,' Pilar says when we get to her house. 'Me first.'

We wave to her until she gets inside.

'Dylan's house next,' Thea's mom says, looking at us in the rear-view mirror. 'Then MayBe's. Thea, are you coming home with me?'

I don't know what she decides. We get to my house without Thea answering, just looking out the window at the rain and singing softly to herself.

That night I pull the extra blanket up from the foot of my bed. It's not cold enough for the winter comforters yet, but the rain's made it damp enough for two blankets.

They still haven't made the news announcement about the metal shavings, and I haven't talked to the deputy since that day in her office. I wonder if maybe they were wrong, maybe the shavings aren't a match. That's what it seems like right now. It just seems unbelievable that it's the Drifter who killed Tessa. That he's come back. I feel so safe, so warm under the covers, the rain tapping against the window, my mom in the next room. How could he be back, if things feel so good?

I fall asleep to the sound of the rain's heavy *thunk-thunk-thunk*. I go back to the desert, and the *thunk-thunk-thunk* turns to *tap-tap-tap*. Sand against the barrel. *He's not back*, I think in my dream, and I'm not afraid. If the deputy wants me to look again, I'll look again. I'm not going to see anything new. *I'm not afraid*, I say aloud in my dream. I look at the barrel first. I crouch next to it. I don't think about what's inside. The adhesive from the peeled-off sticker is peppered with stuck sand. I run my fingers over it, the sand falls off, and I look closer. There is a corner of the sticker that wasn't torn off. There is a stroke of blue, the edge of a circle maybe, or of a letter. I'm looking so closely that I don't notice the footsteps until they stop right behind me. I don't turn around, knowing if I try to, I'll wake up. *What is this?* I ask, pointing to the barrel. There is no answer. *It's not you, though, right?* I try to turn now, twisting hard to my right, and wake up twisting against my mattress.

7

Monday morning I sleep through most of *Good Morning, Sunshine!* and wake up only when my mom marches into my room and pulls the covers off me.

'Third time's a charm,' she says, standing at the foot of my bed. She's already dressed. 'I'm not going to ask you again.'

'What time is it?' I ask with a groan, rolling over to look at the time on my cell phone.

'It's late o'clock, that's what time it is,' she says.

'My head hurts,' I say, putting my hands over my face. 'I didn't sleep at all last night.'

'I can see that's true from the drool on your pillow.'

'I fell asleep at five,' I say, rubbing my eyes.

'Do you need to stay home?'

'No, I'm getting up.'

'Good. Cate's already downstairs, eating all of your Chocolate O's.'

'Did you watch the news this morning?' I ask, sitting

up and rubbing my face.

'Yep, no snow yet. Be quick in the shower, OK?'

My head, leaning against the wall of the shower, feels like it's filled with cotton. My mouth does too, for that matter. It's not entirely true that I fell asleep at five. That's just when I fell asleep for good. After my dream, I spent the night slipping in and out of sleep, jerking myself awake every time I found myself in the desert.

When I get downstairs, my mom and Cate are sitting on the couch watching TV.

'I made you cereal!' Cate says, holding out a bowl toward me.

'Thanks,' I say, taking it and sitting down. I can't decide if this is weird or great, for her to be here at my house before school, eating cereal and watching dumb morning TV with my mom and me. Then I remember she doesn't really have a mom, not one that's around anyway, and I wonder if I'll go to hell for not wanting to share mine.

'OK,' Cate says, when we're at the bottom of the driveway, huddled together under one umbrella, waiting for the bus. 'Are you ready for your daily question?'

'Sure,' I say, yawning. 'Go for it.'

'How does it work?'

'You're going to have to be more specific,' I say. God,

I wish I could just go back to bed. I wonder if I'd have nightmares if I slept on the couch.

'OK, but it still counts as one question.'

'Whatever.'

'Does Deputy Pesquera – that's her name, right? Does she call you when there's a kid missing to see if you can help find them?'

'Nope.'

Cate looks at me.

'Sorry, that was your answer. No more till tomorrow.'

'Oh, come on!' We both wave to Dottie as she drives by.

'I'm joking,' I say. 'Um, OK. I actually call her. Like, with that little girl Angela, I was sitting in homeroom talking to Pilar and all of a sudden I felt this, like . . . splitting in my brain. Like a giant crack right between my eyes that hurt so bad I sort of stopped breathing. All I could hear was the sound of my own heart beating, and even though I could see Pilar in front of me, kicking Frank's chair and putting a pile of green Sour Patch Kids on my notebook, I couldn't hear her, and it felt like she couldn't hear me or see me, like I'd become invisible. And then instead of Pilar, I was seeing . . .'

I stop.

'What? What did you see?'

I don't answer, hoping to see the bus come back into view.

'Oh, come on!' Cate says, stamping her foot. 'You never tell me what you saw. That's no fair.'

'No fair?' I ask, almost laughing in disbelief at the way she's acting. 'Cate, it'd be *no fair* if I told you really private details about the most horrible moment –'

'No fair to who?' she asks stubbornly. 'You already told the police.'

'It'd be no fair to the kids who died,' I say, sad and exasperated that she doesn't understand. 'These aren't my stories to tell. The details . . . they're personal. Private. If I tell you, then it's like gossiping.'

Cate is quiet for a moment. 'I guess I never really thought of it like that. Like gossiping.' She wrinkles her nose and whispers, her voice tight, 'I don't want to be a gossip.'

'I know you don't,' I say. 'But some of the questions you ask . . .'

When she looks at me, she looks almost desperate. She squeezes my arm. 'OK,' she says, 'OK, please let's act like it didn't happen. Like I didn't even ask. I'm so . . . I'm so embarrassed, Dylan.' She's crying now. 'I didn't mean to

163

ask those questions, I didn't mean it. I'm not . . . I'm not a bad person.'

'I know you're not,' I say, the frustration still running through my voice. I take a deep breath. 'I know you're not.'

She sniffs, and tucks her chin into her coat. She looks so small. 'What was it like,' I ask, 'at your old school?'

'Well, first of all,' Cate says, her face brightening, 'it was an all-girls school. We were, like, required *by law* to wear knee socks every day.'

We get on the school bus and Cate spends the ride telling me about her old school. About their plaid skirts and practical jokes, the nuns who were nice and the ones who were '100 per cent pure evil'. I realise then how impossible it is to stay in a bad mood around Cate. How I can't *not* laugh with her when she tells a story, how she has this sort of brightness about her that makes me feel . . . good.

Her answers to my questions always wind their way back to her school, and to stories about the nuns or her friends. By the end of the week, I've heard most of the stories at least once already, but I let her tell them again and again. There's something lonely about it, the way she giggles at the same moment every time she tells a story, and waits a quick second for me to giggle too. I'm not really a giggler; it's actually something Pilar and I have always prided ourselves on. We're more of the hearty-laughter type.

I think my mom likes her too, except that she had to tell Cate to stop coming over so early. One day she showed up before my mom had even gone out running yet, when she was sitting on the couch in her running pants and sports bra.

I find myself happily floating through each day, watching as everyone, even Pilar, warms up more and more to Cate. We bring her over to Thea's so Thea can cut her hair; we bring her to the Niner and we all get stomachaches from eating too many curly fries; we hang out in the village, eating candy and reading magazines in the bookstore.

In the midst of all this, Ben seems to have been initiated into whatever the hell it is Frank and Cray, and even Thea, are up to. When Mr Mueller said Ben had been called to the office with Frank and Cray, Ben practically let out a whoop. They think they're so great because they somehow manage to not leave any evidence. This last time, they broke into some weekenders' houses and peed in the fireplaces. Thea let us in on her secret world long enough to tell us she wasn't there.

I haven't talked to Deputy Pesquera, and I don't care.

They haven't announced anything about those metal shavings, and even though I'm racked by dreams of the desert every night, I spend my days pretending like none of it ever happened. I have this feeling, though, that I'm just biding my time. That the reason all of this is so much fun is that it's all about to change.

Our house is too quiet. Cate said she had to go home and do homework, and Pilar got in a fight with her mom on the phone during lunch and was in a crap mood for the rest of the day. She barely even said goodbye. So it's just me, sitting on the couch, noticing how even with the TV on full volume, it does nothing to fill up the silence.

I last until six o'clock in my empty house, and then leave my mom a message on her cell phone, and head out the door.

I've been going over to Ben's since I was old enough to go anywhere. My mom used to call his mom when I left our house, and they'd talk on the phone the full fifteen minutes till his mom saw me come out of the woods. Then they'd do the same thing on my way home.

It's been dark out for a couple of hours already, and the warm yellow light from inside the Abbotts' barn makes crooked squares on the wet dirt driveway.

I heave open one of the sliding doors to get in the barn, and then close it against the damp and cold. Ben pokes his head out of the stall where he's putting a blanket on Spike, smiles at me, and sneezes.

'Hi,' I say to him, stopping to scratch Marge behind her ears. She thanks me by trying to eat my sweatshirt and marking her efforts with drool.

'Hey, neighbour,' he says, sneezing again, and coming out of Spike's stall and latching the door behind him. Ever since he was a kid, Ben has been allergic to hay. My fantasy of a roll in the hay will never be fulfilled with him at least, without the help of a hefty antihistamine. 'Long time no see. Marge missed you.'

'I can see that,' I say, wiping the slobber from my sweatshirt on to the horse blanket hanging on Marge's stall door. 'How're Tye and JJ?'

'They're lunatics. Can't wait for it to snow. They come down to breakfast every morning in their snow pants and boots and throw tantrums when they see it's raining again.'

'They make you play any Fart Breath lately?'

He laughs. 'Not by choice. You and your mom coming over for Thanksgiving?'

'Yep.'

167

'Good.'

'You going to be there?'

'Where else would I be?'

'With Frank.'

'Frank's a crap cook. I'll be at home.'

'You're just always with him lately.'

'Haven't seen you around much either.'

'I guess I've been busy,' I say.

'Ah, the new friend,' he says, bumping me out of the way by opening Marge's stall door. 'How's that all going?'

'How do you mean?'

He pulls Marge's blanket off the stall door and throws it gently over her back.

'I just mean, you and Pilar.'

'Me and Pilar what?'

'I dunno,' he says from under Marge, where he's fastening the buckles on the blanket. 'You guys don't seem that close any more.'

'We're close!' I say, surprised. 'I still hang out with her all the time.' Or, almost all the time. More and more she's been opting out of our after-school plans, saying she has to go home to babysit. And less and less, I realise, I've tried to stop her.

'Whatever you say.'

'*Whatever.* Did you do water yet?'

Ben shakes his head, finishing Marge's blanket, and says without looking at me, 'She's not one of us, you know.'

'Who, Pilar?' I ask, sarcastically.

He doesn't answer.

'I know she's not.' I rest my hands and chin on the stall door. 'But what's so great about being one of us, anyway? I mean, don't you think it's weird that the thing that makes us all such great friends is a murder that happened eleven years ago? I don't even know if we all like each other any more.'

Ben doesn't answer, just moves me again to open and close the stall door. Something about his stone face makes me turn and walk away, finding the hose coiled in a corner and turning it on.

I drag the hose from stall to stall, cinching it to keep it from leaking as I move, careful not to let the water rush out all at once and spook the horses.

'How's Pesquera?' Ben asks. I look at him, letting the water run over in the bucket I'm filling.

'Shit,' I jump back and cinch the hose. I wipe the spilled water from my jeans before I say, 'What do you mean?'

'I dunno. Cray says he saw you with her. And you're always down at the station.'

'I'm not –' I start to say, but am interrupted by Ben loudly dropping large scoops of feed into the horses' buckets.

The barn fills with the sounds of the horses' noisy eating.

'Just remember who your friends are,' he says.

'That's a crap way to talk to me.' I turn off the hose and roll it back up.

'You have to decide who you're going to be in all this.'

'What the hell is that supposed to mean? In all *what*?'

'You'll see.'

Ben cuts the binding on a bale of hay and we each take half, dropping two sections into each stall.

'What's Frank got you doing?' I say, tossing a section of hay into Marge's stall.

'He doesn't *have* me doing anything.'

'Whatever. What are *you* doing, then?'

He looks at me.

'Jesus, Ben, I'm not a rat.'

He keeps looking at me.

I laugh uncomfortably. 'I didn't rat to your mom about what really happened to her blender in fourth grade, I'm not going to rat now.'

'You've got nothing to rat about.'

'Right. But if I did. I wouldn't.'

He nods. 'OK, then.'

'I'm gonna go.'

'See ya,' he says, turning his back on me to fasten the feed bin. He doesn't turn to watch me leave.

8

'Is this my niece?'

My aunt Ruby's ability to call only when my mom's in the shower or not home is starting to border on annoying. There's only so much of her weird conversation skills that I can take.

'Yep, it's me,' I say, trying not to groan out loud. I just got home from school, and all I want is a giant bowl of cereal, preferably something artificially flavoured. I want to call Pilar too. Even though I see her all the time, it's always with other people. We haven't hung out alone together for weeks. Cate and I, though, have our morning rides to school, and more and more afternoons hanging out at my house.

'What are you *doing*, child?' Aunt Ruby asks, and all of a sudden I feel like a little kid caught with her hand in the cookie jar.

'Um, nothing,' I answer. 'Sitting on my couch. I just got home from school.'

'How's the weather out there?'

'Still raining,' I answer. I tap my fingers against my knees. 'Yep, still raining.'

'I thought it was supposed to snow on that mountain of yours?'

'It is. It's just late this year. Auntie, I have to go,' I say. My stomach rumbles in agreement.

'OK, darling, you go, then. Tell your mama I called.'

'OK. Bye, Auntie.'

The phone rings again as soon as I hang up. It's Pilar.

'Are you watching this?' she asks with an almost hollow voice.

'What?'

'Turn on the TV.'

It's a press conference. Sheriff Dean is standing next to the sheriff from Salvation, who is leaning into a microphone podium, answering a question. Behind them are Deputy Pesquera and a bunch of other cops that I don't recognise.

'The metal fibres seem to be a match to the ones found eleven years ago on Pine Mountain, excuse me, Paradise Mountain.'

The television camera is filming from the back of the room, showing five full rows of reporters with notebooks and tape recorders.

'Do you know what the metal shavings are from?' a woman in the front asks, holding out her tape recorder for the answer.

The Salvation sheriff looks to Sheriff Dean, who steps up to the microphone. 'We believe they are from a machine shop of some kind, one that manufactures finely detailed objects made from light metals.'

'Like what?' the woman asks. 'What sort of finely detailed objects?'

'We don't know,' Sheriff Dean says, stepping away from the microphone.

'Can you believe this?' Pilar asks. 'I don't believe this is happening. We were just talking about this!'

'I know,' I say. 'I can't believe it.'

'The Drifter could be on the mountain right now!'

'I know.'

'Stop saying *I know*!' Pilar snaps. 'Say something real, Dylan. I'm freaking out over here. Say something real.'

'I doubt he's up here,' I say. 'Too much heat.'

She laughs. 'Too much heat. I said *real*, not crime-drama.'

'Well, it's true,' I say, muting the TV. 'There's no way that guy is ever coming back up here.'

'You really think that?' she asks. 'That he won't come back?'

'Sure I do,' I say. The call-waiting tone is actually a relief to hear. 'Pilar, that might be my mom. Hold on.'

'OK, but come back and talk to me. Don't hang up.'

When I switch over to the other line, it's Ben's mom, Mrs Abbott.

'Dylan, is your mom home yet?'

'Nope, she had a late meeting. She said she'd be home around eight.'

'Oh. Are you watching the news?'

'I just turned it on.'

'I just . . . I hate the idea of you up there by yourself. I'm sending Benji up to get you and you'll eat here with us and the twin tornadoes. How's that sound?'

'That actually sounds really, really nice,' I say, running my hands over my arms, trying to calm the goose bumps that seem to be rippling over my entire body. 'Can you hold on a minute?'

I switch back over to Pilar. 'Professor, I'm going down to the Abbotts' until my mom gets home. You're coming too, OK? You and Grace. I'll get his mom to come pick you up.'

'Thanks, Professor,' she says, and then she's quiet for a second. 'Really, thank you. But my mom and dad are pulling in now, so I'm OK. Are you OK?'

'I'm OK. Ben's coming over to walk me down to his house.'

Pilar snorts. 'Your knight in flannel armour. OK, I have to go unbarricade the door so my mom and dad can get in the house. Call me tonight, OK?'

'OK. I love you, Professor.'

'Love you too. Be careful.'

I switch back over to Mrs Abbott and tell her I'm ready to go.

'Great. Ben'll be up in a few minutes. Keep the doors locked till he gets there, and wear your boots, the rain's starting up again.'

'OK, I will.'

My cell phone rings. It's Cate. I don't pick up. Her questions have started to border on the annoying lately, asking for more and more details, especially about Clarence. It's getting so I can't wait for the bus ride to be over every morning. And now, with this. God, she would just freak out.

I leave my mom a message on her cell phone, a note on the kitchen table, and then wait until the doorbell rings. When I get to the door, I look out the window but don't see anybody in the wet darkness outside. My stomach flip-flops. I turn on the porch light and press my forehead against the window.

'Jesus!' I yell when Ben stands up from tying his shoe, appearing suddenly in the window.

'Dude, are you coming or not?' Ben says through the door.

I go outside, locking the door behind me. 'You scared the crap out of me,' I say.

'Sorry. You OK? My mom said you were kind of freaked out.' We circle around to the front of the house and start down the trail.

'I'm all right. Just sort of . . . stunned, you know?'

He nods. 'It's messed up.'

'You got that right.'

We walk in silence for a while, our shoes slushing through the wet grass.

'The boys set you a place at the table already,' he says. 'But I'd avoid using the butter knife they gave you.'

I laugh. 'I'm not going to ask.'

'Good, because they swore me to secrecy. Is that snow?' he asks, stopping and looking up at the cloudy blue-black sky. I do the same, and scream louder than any of us expected when JJ and Tye jump out of the dark woods in front of us. I actually fall over backward and kick out my legs, a move that the boys, including Ben, imitate for their mom as soon as we get inside their farmhouse.

'I'd tell you their torture means they love you,' she tells me, taking my coat, 'but I think it might just mean they're evil.' She pulls me into a hug and whispers into my ear, 'Don't use the fork they gave you.'

My mom comes in as we're finishing dinner. JJ and Tye's disappointment at the fact that I wasn't using any of the silverware they set out especially for me totally disappears when I teach them how to eat spaghetti without a fork, using only their fingers and slices of bread.

'Did any of that get in your mouth?' my mom asks, laughing at my spaghetti-covered face.

'Dylan, come play Fart Breath!' JJ says, grabbing my hand and pulling as hard as he can.

'Yeah,' Tyler says. 'You have to close your eyes and guess if somebody's breathing on you or if they're –'

'I get it, I get it,' I laugh. 'How about I read you a bedtime story instead?'

They answer with an earsplitting 'Yes!'

Mrs Abbott sends them upstairs to change into their pj's and brush their teeth, and I go into the downstairs bathroom to wash the spaghetti off my face. When I come out, my mom and Mrs Abbott are sitting next to each other at the kitchen table, both of them with wet eyes.

'Ben's gone on up to help you,' Mrs Abbott says.

'OK,' I say, hesitating by my mom's chair.

'We're OK, darling,' she says. 'We just need to do some talking.'

'About the Drifter?' I wonder if, in my own head, my voice will ever sound older than five years old when I say his name.

'Go on up,' my mom says. 'We'll talk when we get home.'

But we don't actually talk when we get home. Mom says she's tired, asks if I'm all right, but she's already closing the bathroom door behind her before I can answer.

'Scoot over,' I whisper to her later that night, nudging her with my knee until she makes room for me under the quilt on her bed. I just can't take a visit to the desert tonight.

She takes one of the pillows from under her head and pushes it toward me. 'Your feet are freezing!'

'Aunty Ruby called,' I whisper.

'When?'

'Tonight, before I went over to Ben's.'

Mom yawns. 'What'd she say?'

'I don't know. Why's she so weird, Mom?'

'She's not weird, honey. She's just Ruby.'

'You don't think she's a little strange?'

Mom sighs. 'I know, darling, I know,' she says, reaching out to try to pat my shoulder but poking me in the nose instead. For some reason this makes me laugh really hard, which makes my mom laugh really hard, and we don't fall asleep for a long, long while.

Cate barely waits for me to close my front door the next morning before she asks, 'Did you know about those metal shavings they found?'

'Is that your question of the day?' I ask darkly. I don't feel like doing this with her today. I want my secret back; I want it to be my own again.

'Um, I guess. Yeah. Did you know?'

I don't answer her till we're standing at the end of the driveway. 'Yeah, I knew.'

'Why didn't you tell me?'

'You didn't ask.'

'But we're supposed to be friends. We're supposed to tell each other everything!'

'But why, Cate? Why do you want to know about this stuff? It's *awful*, and I don't know why you can't just let me forget about it!'

'Because,' she says, 'I just want to understand.'

'Understand *what*?'

'You.'

'Cate.' I'm almost begging. 'Don't you see? Everything is going to change now. He's back. Maybe not here, but he's close. And this whole mountain is going to freak out, just like last time. You don't know what it was like, everybody suspecting everybody else, waiting for an announcement that some other kid's been taken.'

'But what if you could stop him?' she asks. 'What if you could figure out who he was?'

'How am I going to do that, Cate? I've never seen him. I *don't* see him!' I'm crying now, thinking about all those nights in the desert, all those nights spent trying to turn around and see who's behind me. I know now that it's him, and that no matter how hard I try, I can't see who he is.

'OK,' she says, patting my arm. 'It's OK.'

'Everything's going to change now.'

9

When we get to school, the Drifter is all anyone can talk about. There's this sort of giddy fear that's overtaken everyone, their conversations sounding less like they're discussing a serial killer and more like they're discussing the prom. Cate heads for her locker at the other end of the hall, and I find Thea sitting on the floor, next to my locker, her head tipped forward as she bites her nails.

One night a few years ago, when we were maybe twelve, Thea showed up on our front porch. It was early spring, still cold enough for me to be wrapped in a blanket in front of the woodstove, drying out from the heavy cold rain that had started on my walk home from the Abbotts' barn. My mom was the one to answer the door when Thea knocked. I remember the feeling of standing up, still wrapped in the blanket, and taking a few steps so that I could see who my mom was talking to. I stopped when I saw Thea, soaked and shivering, haloed by our front porch light, her arms crossed tightly across her chest, the tendrils of her then long-hair plastered against her face. I was afraid. Not of Thea, but of the chaos she brought to our doorstep. I was afraid it would rip out the anchor that held my mom's and my life in place, the anchor of having a schedule, a way of doing things that became as much a shelter to me as our house did. We had closed ranks after my dad left, managed to clumsily seal the rupture of his leaving with stitches made from always having chicken on Wednesday nights and cleaning our rooms on Saturday mornings. I spent the next hour sitting on our couch, staring at Thea's back where she sat wrapped in my blanket, in front of the woodstove. Thea slept over that night, ate our Wednesday chicken and helped my mom with the dishes. She slept on the air mattress in my room, wishing me a good night but saying nothing else. She took the bus to school with me the next morning, and we never talked about it again.

'MayBe's late,' Thea says, not looking up from her nails.

'Pilar, too,' I answer, sitting down next to her.

'You need another haircut,' Thea says, pulling my head toward her, looking closely at my scalp, and then pushing me away. 'You should let me shave it this time.'

'Maybe for summer. Too cold now.'

Thea shrugs and goes back to her nails. 'Whatever.'

'Seriously,' I say, grabbing her hand before she can peel off what's left of her nails. 'Summertime we'll shave it.'

A cluster of first-year girls passes by us, a confused knot of shoulders and elbows pressed together, hurrying down the hall. One of them declares in a hushed voice, 'The older kids call him the Drifter.'

'God, it's like hearing people talk about a movie,' Thea says after they pass. 'Like it's not even really happening.'

'It's not, really,' I answer. 'I mean, it's not happening to them. Not the way it is to us.'

'You're right. Lucky bastards.'

'Seriously lucky,' I agree.

'I'm glad you were here this morning,' she says, getting up and offering me her bit-down hand. I take it, and let her pull me up.

'Me too.'

Cate shows up at my locker as the homeroom bell rings. A moment later Pilar and MayBe come hurrying down the hall with a crowd of kids from their bus route.

'Our stupid bus was late,' Pilar says.

'Superlate,' MayBe agrees.

'Are you OK?' All of us, except for Cate, ask it at the same time. Cate asks the question a moment after, rushing

184

out her words so they sound like an over-anxious echo.

Pilar answers for everyone, 'I'm freaking out.'

We all agree. 'Me too.'

'I mean, he's back, right?' MayBe asks. 'That's basically what Sheriff Dean was saying on the news last night . . . the Drifter's back.'

We hear Frank before we see him, his heavy footfalls running toward us and making us jump. He grabs Thea around the waist and spins her. '*Drifter, Drifter's gonna gettcha!*'

'Not funny!' Thea says, shoving Frank away, just in time for Mr Mueller to step angrily into the hall and warble, 'Ladies and Gentlemen! Do not make me give you detention!'

We file into homeroom, followed by Ben and Cray.

Mr Mueller waits until we're seated. 'Due to the . . . circumstances, we are having extended homeroom this morning to ensure that roll call is properly reported by each homeroom. Please raise your hand and say "here" when I call your name.'

After roll call Mr Mueller picks up the classroom phone and calls down to the office. He tells us to work quietly at our desks until the bell rings.

'Pesquera better hope she catches the Drifter before

we do,' Frank whispers as soon as Mr Mueller opens a book at his desk. What Frank says works as some kind of cue, and in a moment we have all turned our chairs to face one another, a crooked and broken circle. Cate doesn't turn her chair at first. She bites her lower lip and flips through a notebook. After a moment though, she shifts in her chair so she is facing us.

I know what we are about to do, and I have the same jumpy feeling in my stomach I got before the first time we all played spin the bottle in Ben's barn, a squishy feeling of excitement and dread. We are about to tell the story.

'Why? What are you going to do?' Thea asks, spitting a nail in Frank's general direction.

'Kill him,' Frank says, matter-of-factly. 'Slowly.'

'Mountain justice,' Ben says, and Frank nods.

'Idiots,' Pilar says.

'What? You don't think that guy deserves to have his heart ripped out through his . . .' Frank says.

'Oh, please,' Thea snaps. 'You guys want to be old mountain, right? Live up there in the woods crapping in an outhouse and living off chipmunks and wildflowers? You want to bash his head in with an old mountain rock?'

'You said it, babe,' Frank says, 'not me.'

'I'm sorry,' Cate says, speaking for the first time, 'but what's "old mountain"?'

I'm the only one to look at Cate. Everyone else completely ignores her. They ignore her, but wait for me to answer. Like she's my responsibility. She's the outsider that I brought inside.

'It just means the logging families that lived up here before our parents,' I say. 'They all live way up-mountain now. You see them sometimes, in the village, buying supplies or whatever.'

'Oh,' Cate says.

'"Old mountain" says *we* take care of our own,' Ben says, jutting out his chin.

'"We"'? I say. 'Last time I checked, Ben, you had indoor plumbing and all your teeth.'

'Don't be mean,' MayBe says. 'Some of those old mountain people can't afford dental care.'

'And some of them think dentists are government agents come to steal their moonshine,' Pilar says.

Ben shrugs. 'Old mountain's a way of thinking, not just a way of living.'

Pilar gives a hard-edged laugh. 'Those old mountain guys you look up to so much, they'd laugh their asses off if they heard you talking. "Way of thinking." You sound like a moron.'

'Pilar,' MayBe says, trying not laugh.

'What'd I do?' Pilar asks defensively.

'We take care of our own,' Frank says. Cray and Ben nod in agreement.

'God, what does that even mean?' Pilar's almost shouting. '*They* take care of their own. And you aren't one of them. You wouldn't want to be. And they wouldn't want you. You think they were happy when all our parents started moving up here? We ruined their way of life, and now the flatlanders are doing the same to us, and we have no right to complain.'

'Whatever,' Ben says. 'When our folks came up here, they didn't shit giant houses all over the land.'

There's a long pause before I say, 'What does that mean?'

The laughter breaks the tension.

Ben blushes. 'You know what I mean.'

'I'm sorry, man,' Frank says, laughing still, 'but I don't.'

'But . . .' Cate starts to speak, but swallows back her words when this time everyone turns quickly to face her. Pilar doesn't even stifle an annoyed sigh.

'But what?' Frank asks.

'But . . . don't you think that maybe the . . . Drifter . . .

is one of those old mountain people?'

'Oh my gosh,' Thea says with faux earnestness, 'Dean and Pesquera never even thought of that! You've solved the case! Hooray!'

'They tested them all,' I say.

'There's really only two families left up there,' MayBe says. 'And none of the men were a match.'

'Oh,' Cate says quietly.

'Yeah, "Oh",' Pilar grumbles.

'Do you remember how it started?' Pilar asks, like always. This is how the story starts, and now there is no stopping it. We'll tell it like we always do, each of us with the parts that only we tell, the questions only we ask. The only thing different now, though, is that Cate is here.

'It started with Frogger, with Clarence, in kindergarten,' MayBe says. We all nod.

Ben chimes in, right on cue. 'I thought he had just got lost again.'

'He could get lost on the way out of a bathroom stall,' Frank says, not unkindly.

We all nod. The times before, when Clarence hadn't shown up to our kindergarten class, we would clamour over one another with hands raised to get picked for the adventure of finding where he'd gone. Whoever got picked would then have a triumphant return, holding Clarence's hand, and announcing with an almost parental tone of frustration and love that he'd been talking with the cafeteria ladies, or that he'd been in the art room, or he'd been in the janitor's closet. Clarence would stand in front of the class and smile, totally thrilled with the attention.

'Mrs Fenderson sent you, right?' Thea asks Frank, knowing the answer.

'Yeah. Miss Donna called the office, and Dylan came with me because . . .'

Everybody turns and looks at me expectantly.

'Because I blew chunks,' I finally say, and there are small smiles in return; people remembering when barfing in class could count as something truly awful. It won't be my turn again to talk for a while, and I sink into my own memories of that day in kindergarten as my friends recount theirs.

The nurse's office was right next to the main office, and since the nurse was at the high school for the morning, the school secretary, Fran, was the one to have me lie down on the cot with a cool cloth on my head. She left the door between the nurse's office and the main office open.

'No, he's not here,' Fran said when she called Clarence's mom. 'We've checked. Was he feeling OK this morning? Could you just do me a favor and check around your house?'

I could hear more people gathering around Fran's desk. I guess she had covered the receiver with her hand because she was saying, 'His mom is checking. Did we check the closets yet?'

Mrs Madea, the principal, answered. 'They're checking now. Let's delay the bell and keep everyone where they are. Marty,' she said, and I guessed she was talking to the guidance counsellor, Mr Jemson. 'Bring Frank back to class and then go classroom to classroom. I want all teachers to know we have a child missing and to keep their kids in class until we say differently.'

'He's not there?' Fran was talking into the phone again. 'OK. Now I need you to stay put. We're still looking here and we're checking the school buses too.'

Fran called Clarence's name again over the intercom, and the air in the office thickened and crackled with every minute that went by with Clarence not answering.

'I'm calling Sheriff Dean,' Fran said, and nobody disagreed.

When she got him on the phone, she said, 'Sheriff

Dean, it's Fran at the elementary school. Clarence Lacie didn't come to school today. His mom said he left the house, and he's just not here, and he's not at home, either.'

I'd never met Sheriff Dean or Deputy Pesquera before that day. They peeked into the nurse's office, and Sheriff Dean winked at me. 'Headache?' he asked. They both had their hands resting on the guns in their holsters, and from where I lay they looked impossibly tall and almost alien in their uniforms. Sheriff Dean stayed in the doorway while Deputy Pesquera looked under the cot I was lying on, and in the cabinet in the corner.

'Feel better,' Sheriff Dean said, before walking out of the room.

They forgot about me the rest of the day, and I fell into a heavy hot sleep. When I woke up, it was late afternoon, my mom was in the office, and Fran was thanking her for coming down. My mom was someone you called in times like this. She was telling Fran she'd use the cafeteria, and to send the volunteers there to register. While I'd slept, the police had found Clarence's green glasses smashed by the side of the road, and the beanie hat he always wore to hide his lumpy head.

'Well, hello,' my mom said as she glanced into the nurse's office. 'Fran, you didn't tell me Dylan was here.'

Her voice had a soft punishment in it. She came in and sat next to me on the bed.

'Oh my goodness!' Fran almost screamed. 'I forgot. I can't believe it, I just . . .' She practically pushed my mom out of the way to stand next to my cot. 'Dylan, are you OK?'

My mom put her hand on my forehead. 'You're not warm.' Was she lying? I was burning up right in front of her.

'Fran, will you be here for a while?' Mom asked.

I was to stay in the office, now with Fran popping her head in every few minutes and saying 'I forgot she was there' to anyone who'd listen.

My dad took off work the rest of the week to stay home with me, so my mom could run things down at the school. My dad. He is here in this memory, like the cool side of the pillow.

They found Clarence three days later. It was MayBe's mom, leading the deep-woods search team, who saw his little hand in the snow. 'Bare little fingers,' she had said. 'Not even a mitten.'

'My mom found him,' MayBe is saying to Ben.

He answers, 'In the woods, right?'

MayBe swallows. 'In the woods. She could see the edge of his hand. She said it was almost lit up in the sun.'

'Like his glasses,' Frank says, gravely.

'Yeah, I guess. Lit up like his glasses.'

We have a communal threshold for pain, and when we get to the part about Clarence's hand lit up in the sun, we've reached it.

It's time for Cray to turn to me and say the only thing he ever says when we tell this story: 'And you slept through the whole damn thing.'

I'm the little sister in this, the one who slept through Christmas, who played with the box instead of her present, who thought the moon was made of cheese, who asked the librarian why she smelled like feet. My role in this story we tell again and again is to make my friends laugh, to break the tension, and as they look at me with laughing but desperate eyes, I do.

I croon, 'I ate bad candy! I couldn't help it!'

They laugh at this, even if it's not funny, and so they won't be laughing *at me*, I laugh too. Their laughter is my punishment for not being there when the principal came into their class and whispered in Mrs Fenderson's ear and made her cry. For not being there when everyone's parents came early to pick them up from school. For missing the most important part of our shared childhood. I'm one of them and I should have been there in that classroom with them when they realised something was really, really wrong. Of course it's not my fault. But I take the punishment that they think is because I wasn't there, but I know it's because I was there in a way I'll never be able to tell them.

'Oh my *gosh*,' Cate says later that day, when we get off the bus in the village and head toward her apartment. 'That was just crazy.'

'What?'

'This morning. With all of you telling the story about Clarence. It felt like . . . like I was *there*.'

I don't say anything; I just wait behind her as she punches a code into the heavy iron gate that blocks the apartment complex's driveway. The gate swings open, and we walk in.

'And just knowing,' she says, 'what was really happening with you, right at that moment. I can't believe that none of them knew.'

The apartment Cate shares with her dad is nicer than most houses I've ever been inside, including Pilar's. It has super-plush carpeting and fancy kitchen appliances and polished counters and overstuffed furniture that's not mismatched.

'None of this stuff is ours,' Cate says, dropping her backpack on to the couch and motioning for me to do the same. 'Our stuff's all in storage back east until we build the new house. Do you want something to eat?' I follow her into the kitchen. 'I wish Newman was here, but he's out at the house site with my dad. You'd like him, even if he's a fart-a-holic.' She laughs. 'Newman, I mean! Not my dad. My dad just burps. This is us,' she says, taking a picture off the shiny new refrigerator. It's the only thing on the refrigerator, held there by a magnet reading *Patrick Pharmaceuticals, Taluga County*. There's something familiar about that name, but I don't know what it is. I think how the picture looks kind of lonely on the fridge, compared to ours at home, with its layers of Chinese food menus and report cards from when I was seven.

In the photograph, Cate and her dad are standing at the edge of the Grand Canyon wearing matching *That's One Big Canyon!* T-shirts and grinning for the camera. I can tell her dad is holding the camera himself, his arm stretched out in front of them to make them both fit into the image. Cate's dad's hair is even redder than hers, and he wears giant black sunglasses. There is something familiar in their faces that I never noticed just looking at Cate. Something in the sharp point of their chins, the freckles that on her dad have deepened to a warm brown.

'We took that on the way out here,' Cate says. 'We were going to stop at every landmark or silly roadside attraction we could find, but my dad really wanted to get out here. I practically had to beg to get him to stop at the Grand Canyon. He has to wear those stupid sunglasses, even in winter. Sensitive eyes,' she says, rolling her own.

'So what's your dad do?'

She laughs. 'Good question. I mean, I know his title – Senior Vice President of Manufacturing Operations – but I don't even think *he* knows what it means. All I know is some days he has to wear a suit, and some days he wears work boots and jeans because he has to *walk the floor*, which I think means he walks around the plant where they make these little electrical widgets to make sure that the thingamabobbers are being filed down to right size so they can fit into the doohickeys. *So*,' she says, taking a deep breath and giggling, 'your guess is as good as mine.'

I hand the picture back and take the glass of soda she just poured. 'You guys look alike,' I say. 'Same freckles.'

She groans. 'I know. I'm destined to look like a five-year-old till I'm a senior citizen.'

'Your place smells so *clean*,' I say, realising that because of the absence of any sort of odour, I can actually smell the soda we're drinking.

'I know. I hate it,' she says, laughing. She looks around the room, a lost expression on her face. 'It just doesn't smell like *home*, you know? Not like your house.'

'Um, thanks?'

'You know what I mean!' She laughs again, pinching me lightly. 'Your house always smells like cereal and the wood stove and the shampoo from your shower. It smells like people actually live there. Want to see my room?'

Cate's room is enormous. 'This place actually has two master bedrooms, so I have my own bathroom and fireplace,' she says, 'which is really romantic for me and Newman.'

Cate goes into the bathroom, and since there's nothing to look at on the walls or the bookshelves or even the bedside table, I sit on one of the overstuffed armchairs by the fireplace. This place is so quiet, even with the low hum from the bathroom fan. It feels . . . lonely. I see the corner of a book sticking out from under Cate's bed. I don't know why I walk over and pick it up, I just do.

It's a photo album, stuffed so full its yellowing pages fan out, even when closed. When I pick up the book, a piece of paper slips out of it and flutters to the floor. I lay the album on the bed and bend over to pick up the piece of paper.

'What are you doing?' Cate asks, stepping quickly from the bathroom.

'Wait,' I say, glancing at a familiar image on the paper as she snatches it from me. 'What is that?'

'Nothing.'

She tries to slip the paper back into the album, but I grab hold of the edge of it before she can. For a moment we stand there, looking at each other, each holding one end of the paper.

'Let me see it,' I say, pulling a little. 'Cate, let me see.'

She lets go of the paper and leans heavily against the bed.

'Where did you get this?' I ask.

She shrugs. 'Online. It's just a printout.'

I look again at the paper in my hand. The article is ten years old, from the *Pine Mountain Gazette*. It has a picture of Clarence, the same one from my photo album. The headline says *Missing Boy Found Dead*. I don't read the article. I hand it back to Cate, and without opening the album on the bed, she slips it back inside, still leaning against the bed.

'Why –'

She interrupts me. 'Because I wanted to know.'

'Know *what*?' I lean next to her on the bed.

'To know what happened. What it was like for you guys. I mean, you don't understand. What happened obviously cinched you all together in a way that I'll just never be a part of . . .'

'Cate, you wouldn't want to be a part of it.'

She looks at me and gives me a sad smile. 'I like you. All of you. And I just thought that maybe if I understood what it is that made you all so sad . . .'

'We're not sad.'

She laughs ruefully. 'Maybe not all the time, maybe not on the surface, but you and MayBe and Thea and Pilar, even the guys. There's a sadness that you don't think you show. But I can see it. I thought maybe if I understood what it was like for you guys, then we'd all be better friends. I'd be more a part of the group.' She flops back on to the bed and stares at the ceiling. 'I know how it looks. Like I'm sort of freakily obsessed or something. I'm not, though. I'm just tired of being on the outside.'

I move from the bed and curl into the overstuffed chair, tucking my legs beneath me and resting my head on the chair arm. For a long time there is only the sound of us breathing. 'I'm sorry if you feel like you're on the outside,' I finally say.

'It's OK,' she says. 'I know you guys don't mean it.'

'You just came up here at a weird time.'

'I know. I wish I'd moved here a long time ago, so we could have all been little kids together. I wish I'd had my sixth birthday at the Niner, I wish I'd got kicked out of Girl Scouts with you and Pilar, I wish I could have had the chance to go over to MayBe's with you guys and make up recipes for shampoo in the blender.' She sits up and wipes her eyes. 'I guess I just feel like I missed out, is all.'

'You're exhausting,' I say, my head still on the chair.

She laughs a little. 'I know! My dad is always telling me that I wear him out.'

I sit up. 'I see what he means.'

'Are we still friends?' she asks.

'Yes. No.' I laugh, shaking my head. 'I don't know. I don't know if we can be friends if you can't let this thing with Clarence go. It's too much, to keep talking about it. Especially now. Especially since –'

'The Drifter's back?' she asks brightly.

I groan. 'Yes, especially since the Drifter's back.'

'You could catch him, you know,' she says.

I bang my head a few times against the soft arm

of the chair. 'Why are we still talking about this?'

'Because you're scared. I bet you could see lots of things, if you'd just let yourself.'

I think about my dream, the same dream again and again, the same details that tell me *nothing*. 'I wish you were right.'

'Me too,' she says, almost too softly for me to hear.

We walk down to the lake, to the beach I used to go to as a kid but haven't seen since they put the gates up. It's raining, but I've always liked the beach in the rain. We walk up and down the beach until we're totally soaked, and then go back into Cate's apartment and sit by the big fire – which you 'light' by flipping on a light switch – to dry off.

10

On the rainy walk to the bus stop a few days later, Cate tells me she's taking us all on a field trip after class. The sky is low and dense with white, but the flakes still refuse to fall.

'Frank can drive us,' she says. 'I already asked him.'

When we meet at Frank's truck after school, Ben, MayBe, Thea, and Cray are there, but not Pilar. All day I've been trying to track Pilar down, but during homeroom she was in the nurse's office with a headache, and then at lunch she was finishing a lab for bio.

'Where's Pilar?' I ask. It's so weird, to be asking the whereabouts of someone who's usually standing right next to me.

'She didn't want to come!' Cate says, like she's amazed. I try to remember if I talked to Pilar about coming with us. Have I even talked to her at all today?

When we pull out of the parking lot, we see Pilar waiting for her bus. Frank honks and we all wave. She waves back and I crane my head trying to catch the look on her face as she watches us drive away. I feel like I am in the wrong place: I should be with her, going wherever she's going, not in this packed truck that smells like oil.

'Where are we going?' I ask, hoping the answer will be a place I can find an excuse for not wanting to go to.

'I told you, it's a surprise for everybody!' Cate says.

Cate gives directions, leaning over and speaking low into Frank's ear. We drive to the south side of the mountain, and up an unfamiliar long street with faded and cracking pavement. I realise my house is over the ridge.

'Oh my God,' Thea says. Cray pats her knee. The street ends in a cul-de-sac, a wide circle edged by seven houses with darkened windows and empty driveways. They aren't the usual mountain houses. High and narrow with small windows, it's like they are lying in wait. Or standing guard.

'Nobody lives here any more,' Cate says. 'My dad is building our house up here after they tear everything down.'

She finally notices the silence that's come over us all. 'What's wrong with you guys?'

'I haven't been up here for years,' MayBe says, 'not since I came with my mom to drop off a casserole.'

Frank looks at Cate for a long moment and then says, 'This is the old Croondon settlement.'

'Yeah, that's what my dad says. What's that mean?' she asks, confused.

'It was a whole extended family that lived up here,' MayBe says with a sigh. 'From Delaware or someplace like that. They bought this land together and paid to get the road paved, and then spent months building each other's houses.'

'Why'd they move out?' Cate asks. 'Dad says they left plates on the tables, laundry on the line, like they all just walked outside to look at a rainbow and kept on walking.'

Nobody says anything.

'So why'd they move?' she asks again.

'Because Clarence was a Croondon,' Cray says from the back.

'Clarence . . . I thought his last name was Lacie?'

'Lacie was his stepdad's name,' Thea says. 'I don't know what his real dad's name was. Croondon was his mom's maiden name. They were all sisters, all the Croondons; most of them kept their names, even when they got married.'

It's weird, how when someone dies, you fall into this never-ending process of *really* realising they're gone forever, that there is a whole lifetime's worth of conversations you'll never have with them. If Clarence were still here, he and I could talk about how we both come from families where the moms kept their maiden names and about how weird the term *maiden name* actually is.

Frank opens the door and gets out. He looks back into the car at Cate. 'You got us here. Now what?'

'I'm so sorry,' she says, as Ben gets out too. That familiar wrinkle is creasing her chin. 'I didn't know . . . I thought . . . I thought we'd just go in and look because it's so . . . spooky.'

Frank and Thea. She climbs on to his back, and he carries her that way to where Cray and Ben are standing. MayBe gets out next, leaving just Cate and me. Cate looks at me. 'I swear, Dylan, I didn't know. We should just leave. Will you get them back in the truck?' she asks.

'We're here now,' I say, climbing out. She gets out after me. We stand in a clump, nobody talking, us looking at the houses, and the houses looking back at us.

Frank raises his eyebrows at MayBe.

'It was that one,' she answers, pointing to a house that was probably once a pretty shade of blue. Frank starts walking.

'We don't have to go in!' Cate calls after him, but everyone's following him already. She looks at me for a moment and then, with a sigh, follows too. I stand alone. The stillness of the houses seems purposeful, like just a moment ago they were leaning over and whispering into one another's front doors. I hurry into the house.

Cate's right. They did leave everything behind. The musty smell is overpowering. I can smell the dampness of the rotting couches, the molding rugs, and the dust caked on top of the picture frames. From the front entry I can see into the kitchen. On the counter is a plate mounded with something grey, and five plastic glasses stacked neatly beside it.

'Where are you guys?' I call.

'Up here.' I follow Thea's voice to the top of the staircase, where everyone is gathered outside an open bedroom door, their eyes all focused on something inside the room. I lean in to see what they're looking at. The faded mural covers the whole wall, a jungle with tree frogs and panthers and monkeys and Clarence's name spelled out in vines.

Frank's the first one who steps inside the bedroom, and almost immediately Ben is slapping him on the back saying 'It's all right, man, it's OK' at Frank's ragged sobs. MayBe cries openly. So does Thea, Frank's arm wrapped around her. Even Cate has tears streaming down her face.

I'm the only one still standing in the hallway. Cate reaches out her hand from inside the bedroom, and I let her pull me inside. Almost immediately I drop her hand and step away from her, glaring at her. I can't believe this. The sniffling around me stops.

'You all right, Dylan?' Frank asks.

'She didn't know, Dylan,' MayBe says. 'She didn't know this is where he lived.'

I'm still staring at Cate. I try to hold my words in, but they hiss out. 'He died in this room.'

Frank starts bawling all over again, and Ben says, 'Shut up, no he didn't. He died in the woods.'

MayBe looks at me. 'No. Remember. The woods are where they found him. But maybe it happened somewhere else.'

'How did you know that?' Thea asks me, her hands making soft circles on Frank's back.

Cate looks at me, terrified. At first I think it's because she knows the position she's put me in, but then she says, 'That's not true, is it, Dylan? He didn't die here, right?'

I look helplessly at my friends and then manage to sputter, 'M-my mom . . . Sheriff Dean told her,' I say.

'When? When did he tell you? I mean *her*?' Cray asks harshly.

'Last week,' I lie. 'They were talking about those metal shavings and he said . . .'

I look at the window and the image flickers and brightens until the window I am seeing is not broken and caked with dirt, it is whole and clean with neatly painted trim. I turn to my right, ready to ask Cate if she sees what I'm seeing. But she's not there. Instead I see the mural on Clarence's wall, its colours still bright and fresh. There is a neatly made-up roll-away bed against the mural. I look back to the window. Outside, snow is falling. The window opens, and first snowflakes come rushing in, sprinkling the green with white, and then comes a heavy black boot that scuffs the wall and presses mud into the carpet, the leg and body it is attached to working their way through the window. 'The guy actually came in through the window,' I hear myself say, watching a man, his legs and body inside the room, huge next to the child-size furniture, stooping down to fit his shoulders and head through the window. His hands push against the sill and, with his back toward me, he is all the way in the room. *Turn around*, I think, *turn the hell around and let me see your face.* I lunge forward, wanting to grab at his shoulders to make him face me, wanting to slam him against the wall, wanting his head to smack against the hard trim of the

209

window, wanting him to feel the fact that he's not so big after all.

'Dylan?'

The broken window, the peeling mural, the matted and mouldy carpet, appear around me. Outside there is no snow. There is no man coming through the window. There are only my friends, watching me with anxious faces.

'You all right?' Thea asks.

I nod.

'So what happened?' Cate asks. 'What happened when the man came through the window?'

It takes me a second to find my voice. 'I don't know,' I say. 'Dean said the Drifter must have done it here, and then taken Clarence out the window. And then everybody in these seven goddamn houses full of people assumed someone else had taken him to school.'

We ride home in silence until Ben squeezes Frank's shoulder and says, in all seriousness, 'You have a good cry, man?'

Of course we all laugh. And when we repeat this story to each other in the future of our lives, we'll all laugh again at Ben's earnest squeeze of Frank's shoulder.

'It's just so morbid. Standing in his room,' Pilar says the

next morning. We're on the bus on our way to her house to babysit Grace.

'Cate says she didn't know,' I say, shaking my head against the memory.

'Well, I'm glad I missed it.'

'I miss *you*,' I say, nudging her with my shoulder.

'I know. Me too,' she says. 'I just need to get caught up.'

'Cate's a whiz at pre-calc,' I say, 'if you need help. She took it last year.'

Something flashes over Pilar's face.

'What?' I ask. 'You like Cate. Right?'

'Yeah, of course I do.'

'But why'd you make that face?'

I think she's just going to deny it, say that she's tired again, but after a second she says, 'Because I miss it being just me and you.'

'It is just me and you,' I say.

'No.' She shakes her head. 'She's got a hold on you.'

'How do you mean?' I'm trying really hard not to sound defensive.

'I just mean that you guys got into this really deep friendship, really fast.'

'Oh, that's just Cate,' I say quickly. 'She's a blabbermouth; it makes her easy to talk to.'

'How come we don't tell each other our secrets, like you guys do?' Pilar asks.

This silences me. The thing I have always liked about my friendship with Pilar is that I know we both have our secrets. I know that there are things with her family that she doesn't tell me about. And I think she knows there's something I keep from her.

'Because that's what makes us *us*. The fact that we keep each other's secrets, even if we don't know them. We keep them by not asking about them.'

She looks at me a long time without nodding. 'I've always liked that about us.'

'Me too,' I say, wanting nothing more than to get off the bus, to get away from the lies I just told, and the person who saw through them.

We don't talk any more about anything. We get to her house and play with Grace, and then my mom comes to pick me up. Pilar's already walking upstairs when I'm putting on my coat to leave. She stops at the upstairs landing and leans on the railing, looking down at me. I try to read the realness of her smile. We say goodbye, and I fight the urge to run out the door. When we were on the bus, she gave me the chance to tell her, and I lied. I can't believe what I've done.

11

I'm in the shower the next morning when the vision comes. I say out loud, 'What?' pressing my palm against the wall to keep myself from falling. 'What?' I say again, my brain feeling brittle, cracking and ripping with the image of a round little chin, a red-and-white-striped shirt stretched out at the neck, and a small red mouth shoved into the dirt.

I'm sitting on the couch with a wet washcloth on the back of my neck when the deputy arrives. My mom is pacing the floor in front of me.

'I don't think she should go,' my mom is saying.

'OK,' the deputy says, 'that's your choice.'

'I *know* it's my choice. I'm her mother.'

'I'm going,' I say, standing up. I hand the washcloth to my mom.

'No,' she says firmly, splatting the washcloth back on to my neck. 'You're not.'

'I can't help it, Mom,' I say. 'You know I can't. I'm

sorry if you . . .' my words falter, and I breathe deeply to keep from crying.

'You're sorry if I what, darling?'

'Nothing.' I hand her the washcloth again. This time she takes it.

Deputy Pesquera and I drive down the mountain in silence, until we reach the familiar browns and washed-out greens of the desert.

The deputy turns off the highway as soon as we're down the hill.

I look at her, surprised. 'This close?'

She nods.

'In Taluga?' I ask. 'Where Open Earth is?'

She nods again. 'This is where the company that bought them is. Partridge Pharmaceuticals or something like that.'

'He's getting closer,' I say quietly.

Taluga is practically at the base of the mountain.

A high desk that reaches up to the top of my head blocks our entry when we walk into the station.

The desk sergeant looks down at me, making his fat neck puff out over his collar. 'This her?' he asks.

'Yep,' Pesquera says. The sergeant nods toward a door,

pressing a button to buzz us in. The deputy has her hand on my shoulder and she leads me to the interview room.

There's the usual metal table in the middle of the room and the usual one-way mirror on one wall. Leaning against the mirror is a short blank-faced female officer who, when I come in, looks to the other officer, a short, stubby man with his hands on his hips.

'This her?' The man, who has a wiggly mouth that I instantly dislike, asks.

'Yes, this is Dylan,' Deputy Pesquera says, coming in behind me.

'Hi,' I say.

'I'm Detective Armstrong,' the wiggly mouth says. 'And this is Detective Cronin.' He doesn't even motion to her and she does nothing to acknowledge that he has said her name.

'Hi,' I say again.

'How does this work?' Detective Armstrong asks, like he's already unhappy with the answer. 'Do you see anything?'

'I don't . . .' I look to Deputy Pesquera for help.

'You need to brief her on the case,' the deputy says.

'Fine. Sit down,' Armstrong says, nudging a chair out from under the table with his boot. He sits down across from me and opens the file in front of him. 'Ten-year-old Brian Ferr, missing since yesterday. Sandy-brown hair, last seen wearing blue jean shorts and a red-and-white striped T-shirt, and I think what they say you can do is bullshit.'

'May I?' I reach for the picture of Brian from the file. Armstrong takes it out from under the paper clip and slides it across the table.

'That was taken on school picture day, three weeks ago.'

'He was wearing this same thing when he went missing?' I ask, pointing to the red-and-white shirt in the photo.

'Guess so,' Armstrong grunts.

'Hmm,' I murmur.

'Hmm. That's all you've got, is *"Hmm"*?' Armstrong takes the photo back. 'Is the kid alive or what?'

I look at Deputy Pesquera. She just looks back at me. Big help she is.

'I've only been able to find kids that are . . .' My confidence wavers and I can't finish the sentence.

'Oh, great!' Armstrong says, standing up and crossing his arms. He looks down at me. 'So is he dead? Do you see him being dead?'

'No,' I say.

'So he's alive?' Armstrong says. I could punch him in the crotch from where I sit.

'I don't know. I can't concentrate with you yelling at me.'

'Oh, this isn't yelling, sweetie. This is playing nice. Let's hope you don't have to hear me yell.'

'Does that actually work with criminals?' I ask. I can feel something; I can feel the edge of something in my mind.

'So if you tell us he's near water, no matter where we find him – near a garden hose, the ocean, or a bucket – you get to say you're right, right?'

'I think you should go outside and let us work with her,' Deputy Pesquera says.

'No, this is our investigation. I don't know what kind of mountain-law you practice, but if it happens here, I stay here.'

'Then you'll have to shut up,' I say.

He motions with his hand, a *fine, I'll stop talking* motion. He winks at Detective Cronin. She ignores him.

I look at the picture. Brian's hair is slicked down, the beginnings of a cowlick raising a chunk of hair near his part. I laugh a little.

'What?' Armstrong says. 'This is funny to you?'

'His mom, she used to give him a spit bath to make that part in his hair stay down,' I say.

'What the hell does that have to do with anything?' he says.

'This is how it works,' I say drily. 'I tell you his story, and when we get to the end, we know how it ends.'

'Well, I'll come back when you get to the end,' Armstrong says, heading for the door.

'No,' I say, realising something. 'You have to be here. The fact that you're being a total *prick* is helping; it's . . . it's started something. I have to tell the story to *you*. Sit down.' I kick the chair out from across the table. It's quite possibly the most badass thing I've ever done. Armstrong sits, laughing.

'We'll do this together, you and me,' I say, not letting him look away. 'I know you don't believe me, and that's good. Keep disbelieving.'

He glares at me. 'No problem.'

'The night before this picture was taken,' I say, holding up Brian's photo, 'the kid ironed his own shirt and hung it on a hanger. His brother helped him with the ironing board, setting it up so it was low enough for Brian to reach. His brother put his hand on Brian's and showed him how to smooth out the wrinkles. Brian's brother is a real swell dresser. They put the shirt on a hanger together and hung it on the shower rod. Brian doesn't have his own closet; he has a box under the bed. In the morning his mom comes home from work and Brian is sitting on the couch in his freshly ironed shirt, his cuffed socks, his clean trousers. She tells him he's a handsome boy, kisses him on both cheeks. He catches the bus to school.' I pause. I look at Armstrong. 'There is something green out the window.'

Armstrong looks at the one-way glass window on one side of the room.

'No,' I say. 'There is something green out the window of the bus, and Brian sees it.' I'm starting to cry. 'He goes to school, and sits for his picture, smiling this ridiculously huge smile. Like his eyes disappear under his chubby cheeks. The kid's so cute that everyone laughs – his teacher, the older kids, and the photographer. And after him, all the kids try to give their biggest smiles – just like Brian, they say, and the class pictures come out looking like everyone's on mood elevators. After school he gets on the bus for the ride home.' I clench my fists. 'There's something goddamn green out the window!' I yell. 'Why can't anybody see it?'

Detective Armstrong raises his eyebrows. He's enjoying this.

'Three weeks later – yesterday – Brian wears his picture-day outfit to school again. After school he gets off the bus and walks toward his house, and when he's out of sight of the street . . .' I take a deep breath, seeing the rush of colour as someone grabs Brian's right arm and pulls him, dragging him. I see the torn knees of Brian's little-boy jeans, holes in the fabric rimming with blood. 'Brian thinks, *You're stretching out my shirt*, and he thinks, *My knees are scraping the driveway*, and he thinks, *If I open my mouth wide enough, I can breathe*, and he thinks, *I can't breathe*.'

I can't see the man dragging Brian. I can see only a hint of his posture as he walks purposefully forward, leaning ahead as he walks. As if he were walking through a snowstorm. I've seen that posture before.

'He's taking Brian to . . . There's something green.'

'Who is it? Kermit the frog?' Armstrong asks. I can tell he's trying hard to keep his stupid smirk off his face. 'Can you see who took the kid?'

I look at Deputy Pesquera when I answer. 'It's him.'

'It's *who*?' Armstrong asks. 'And what's the green thing?' He's getting frustrated. I'm afraid he'll walk out of the room, afraid that he won't keep pushing me.

I look at Armstrong. 'Ask me.'

He glares at me.

220

'It's not a game,' I say. 'I don't know that answer till you ask me the question.'

'Who took the kid?'

'The Drifter took him.'

Armstrong blinks. 'What's the green thing?'

'Ask me,' I plead.

'I am!' he barks. 'Is it . . . bigger than a bread box?' he asks. He's sort of enjoying this now, waiting for the payoff so he can show me to be a liar.

I nod.

'Is it on wheels?'

I nod.

'Is it a car?'

I shake my head.

'Truck.'

I pause. 'Yes.'

'Commercial? Or like some mud-covered truck you'd drive up the mountain?'

'It's like a boxy truck.'

'Sounds commercial,' Armstrong says. He studies me for a second, and then says to Detective Cronin, 'See what an APB picks up on a green boxy truck.'

'There is a long road with sharp rocks and they hit the undercarriage – ping, ping, ping.'

'Dirt road?' he asks.

I shake my head. 'Gravel. Like, clean gravel.'

'What else?'

I can see something else. 'Oil? Do you make oil down here?'

He laughs. 'This ain't Texas.'

'Wind. Do you pull wind for energy?' I ask. 'Because there's windmills there, I can tell you that.' I can see more now. 'There's fake water.'

'Water. There we go.' He stands and glares down at me. 'Well, thank you for coming down and wasting my time.'

'A windmill,' I say. 'Like, a non-working windmill. It turns, but doesn't do anything.'

'Could be a minigolf course?' Cronin says.

'No. Say something else.' I lock eyes with her.

'Is there grass there?' Cronin asks, sitting in the chair next to Armstrong. He looks at her, annoyed.

'Real grass, but it looks fake.'

'Fake grass, fake water, fake windmill,' Armstrong says.

I look at him. 'It's like short, spongy grass.'

'Is there a clown? Is it a minigolf course?' Cronin asks again.

'No. But the same sort of grass.'

'Like an office park?' Cronin asks suddenly. 'Do

you know what an office park looks like?'

I nod. A couple years ago we went down to visit the new warehouse where they make Open Earth.

'Let's look at office parks in the area,' Armstrong says. 'Ones with windmills.'

'Oh!' I say. 'You'll see the red from his shirt, he's still wearing it. But it blends in with the red bridge.'

'There's a red bridge?'

'I guess so. Yes.'

'A red bridge and a windmill,' Armstrong says, studying me.

I nod.

He inhales deeply. 'OK. Wait here.'

Deputy Pesquera follows Armstrong and Cronin out of the interview room, leaving me sitting alone at the table. I pull Brian's photograph out of my sleeve, where I'd tucked it earlier, and slip my arm up under my T-shirt. I peel the Band-Aid away from my chest, and slide in the photograph. I press the edges of the Band-Aid back against my skin.

The Drifter leaned forward to drag Brian to the truck, just like he had leaned forward against the wind and snow, just like when he left Clarence in the woods.

*

223

They find Brian in an office park, hidden by the employee picnic table area, which overlooks the decorative windmill and bridge. Employees ate their lunches today, enjoying the warm, dry weather. No one noticed the shock of striped shirt lying in the shadows.

12

'Where were you last night?' Pilar asks. I can't answer for a second, because she looks so wrecked.

'I was . . . out,' I say.

'Liar!' She's in tears. 'I called your house. Your mom said you were sick.'

'That's what I meant,' I say. 'Pilar, are you OK?'

'Did you hear what happened? Down the hill? What the hell, Dylan!' She's clutching her books to her chest, her knuckles white from gripping them so tightly.

'I did hear about it, but that's down the hill. It wasn't up here.'

'Bullshit! Stop lying! Why are you always lying?'

I step back.

'Why do you pretend like everything's OK? It's not OK, Dylan! He's back! He's coming back and you just refuse to admit it!'

'I'm sorry,' I say, reaching out to her. She pulls away from me.

'I'm never going to sleep again, Dylan.'

'Yes, you will,' I say. 'They're going to catch him.'

'Are my eyes abnormally big?' she asks.

'No,' I lie. Her bloodshot eyes are almost bulging out of her head.

'Because they feel big. I haven't slept, Dylan. I can't *sleep*. What if he gets Gracie?' She lets go of her books, dropping them to the floor, and grabs my shoulders. 'What if he gets my Gracie?'

'Hi, guys,' Cate says, coming up behind Pilar. Cate motions to me with her eyes, flicking them off to the side, anxious for us to get away so she can pepper me with questions. This morning, when I called her, I didn't let her talk at all, I just told her not to come over this morning, that I needed some time with my mom.

I ignore the way she's now pulling lightly on the sleeve of my sweatshirt, trying to pull me away, saying, 'Dylan, come with me to the bathroom.'

I move out of her reach, my eyes still on Pilar.

Cate sighs at me and then looks at Pilar. 'Oh my gosh, Pilar, are you OK?'

Pilar is trying not to cry. 'Dylan,' she says.

'Oh, no! Don't cry, Pilar,' Cate says, pulling Pilar into a hug. Pilar resists, trying to push away, but it's like she has

226

no strength, and her arms end up hanging limply at her sides. She collapses against Cate, crying.

Why didn't I think of hugging her?

'I know, I know,' Cate whispers, stroking Pilar's hair.

Pilar is crying, and I can hear that she's saying 'stop'.

Cate looks at me over Pilar's shaking shoulder. Something in Cate's face. Happiness? At what? Being needed?

'Pilar, would you do me a favour?' Cate says, in a voice so comforting it makes my skin crawl. 'Would you come down to the nurse with me? They let you take naps there. Maybe you'll feel better if you get some sleep.'

Cate smiles at me. 'Dylan will come.'

Pilar finally pulls herself away from Cate, and reaches for my hand. Hers is cold. 'OK, let's go.'

'Good girl,' Cate says, taking Pilar's other hand. Pilar doesn't object. I don't think she even notices.

When we get to the nurse, Cate convinces her to let us 'tuck Pilar in'. With Pilar curled under the blanket, looking angry even in her sudden sleep, I go to follow Cate out of the room. Something clenches the back of my leg, and I turn. Pilar's staring at me hard with glassy eyes. 'Stay here,' she says, giving a tug where she's squeezing my leg.

'Oh, OK,' I say. I sit down next to her on the cot. Cate

makes a move to do the same and Pilar wrinkles her lip. 'Not you, princess.'

I look at Pilar, and then at Cate.

'Sure. I have to go to class anyway. Feel better, Pilar,' she says, and I can hear her voice wavering. It's not till she's out of the room that Pilar lets go of my leg and lets her head fall back on to the pillow.

'I can't sleep with all her clucking,' she says, her eyes closed, her face relaxing into a mask of sleep. 'Just sit here.'

'What?'

She wrinkles her brow, but keeps her eyes closed. 'I don't care. Sit here and maybe I'll fall asleep.'

She actually snores. A real, perfectly formed snore that has me clapping my hand over my face to keep from laughing and waking her up. I start to get up and she stirs a little. I'm stuck, which makes me immediately have to pee more than I've ever had to pee in my life. I wait a looooong twenty seconds and then try to get up again. Pilar wrinkles her nose in her sleep. I look up and see the school nurse watching me from where she's doing paperwork at her desk. She comes over and reaches out her hand, saying in a voice I fear is far too loud, 'It's all right. Back to class. She'll be out for a while.' I let her pull me up, and Pilar stirs but doesn't wake. At the entrance to the nurse's office I ask, 'Is she down here a lot?'

She looks at me brightly and doesn't answer. I don't make her recite her oath of nurse-patient privilege. I just leave.

I wake up with a gasp just after two a.m. and reach for the phone.

I dial a number. It rings three times before a sleepy voice answers. 'Hello?'

'I had a nightmare,' I say, my voice sounding small in the dark of my room.

'You did?' Cate whispers. 'About the kid from last night?'

'No. I was walking down the hall of the police station, toward the interrogation room, and there's a mother there, and she sees me walking toward her and somehow she knows that I'm there to see her dead child, and the mother starts screaming and screaming and screaming.'

'Holy crow,' Cate whispers. 'That gave me goose bumps.'

I hold my own arm out into the glow from my alarm clock. 'Me too,' I say.

'That means,' Cate says quietly through a yawn, 'that our goose bumps are psychically connected. What number am I thinking of?'

'It's three in the morning. I can't think of a number,' I say.

'Oh my God!' Cate croaks.

'What? Were you thinking of the number three?'

'No, nine, which is a multiple of three. OK, guess again.'

I stretch out under the covers. 'Ummm, seven.'

Cate's quiet for a second. 'If by seven you mean four, then you're totally right! Guess again.'

'Um . . . four,' I say.

'. . . teen. Fourteen. Totally right again!' she whisper-yelps. 'OK, let me try you. You are thinking of the number . . . ten.'

'Nope.'

'Oh, come on! Eleven?'

'Nope.'

'Four?'

'Nope,' I say, laughing into my pillow.

'Three?' She sighs. 'Onetwothreefourfivesixseven –'

'Seven,' I say.

'Dude,' Cate says quietly, 'I'm totally psychic.'

'Totally.' I giggle. 'I'm going back to sleep.'

'OK, me too. Hey, Dylan?'

'Yeah?'

'Do you dream about them? The kids you've seen?'

Her question makes the dark get darker, and my mom's room seems very far away from my own.

'Sometimes,' I say, propping up on my elbows and pressing one hand against my forehead. Why is she asking this?

'How come you don't talk about them more, then? I mean, to me. You can talk to me about it, you know?'

'I know I can,' I say.

'Good!' she says cheerily. 'See you tomorrow. Happy Friday!'

We hang up and I pull my covers over my head.

At first I thought that Cate would keep my secret. She would tuck it into her heart and hide it, like I do. But she didn't. She is biting my secret in half to see what it is made of.

There's something I didn't tell her, though. I knew what numbers she was thinking of.

13

'Dylan?'

It's been so long since Pilar's called me on the phone, it takes me a second to recognise her voice. It's Sunday afternoon; I haven't seen her all weekend.

'Hey, Pilar! How are you feeling?'

'Can you come over?' she asks, her voice leaden.

'What's wrong?'

'Can you come over?' she asks again.

'Sure, let me just ask my mom.'

'Tell her you have to, just for a couple hours.'

'OK. I'll be over soon.'

'Are you sure she's home?' Mom asks when we get there. All the lights are off. 'It's Pilar, Mom. She's saving electricity.'

'Oh. Don't let her read in that light. She'll go blind.'

'I'll be sure to tell her.'

'Lock the door behind you.'

I don't knock, just let myself in. Pilar is sitting on the

232

couch in the dusky light, Grace asleep beside her, her head resting in Pilar's lap. I sit down, rubbing Grace's little feet.

'Hi, Professor,' I say softly.

'I keep falling asleep,' Pilar says.

'OK.'

'I keep falling asleep, and I can't fall asleep.'

'OK.'

'What do you think it's doing to all of us?' she asks.

'I don't know.'

'I mean, it can't be good, right?' She gives a harsh laugh. 'It can't be good for us to live through this. Do you think it's, like, messing us up? How can we ever be happy knowing these things are happening? How can you live a normal life when you've seen these things? I think it might have done something to me, Dylan. I think that little kid down the hill – I think it did something to me.' She looks at Grace. 'I keep falling asleep,' she says, 'and I can't. I can't fall asleep. You have to sit here, Dylan. You have to sit here and promise me you won't fall asleep. If I sleep now, I can be awake tonight. You have to sit here with us, Dylan.'

'OK.'

'Don't fall asleep.'

'OK,' I say.

'You're the only one I trust, Dylan. You'll stay awake,

right? When I wake up, I won't be so crazy. I just need some sleep.'

'OK.'

'You know what tomorrow is, right?'

'What?'

'Eleven years. Can you believe it? It seems like yesterday.'

'I know.'

'Stop saying . . . ' Her eyes close, and then she shakes her head, opening them again. 'I think I love Gracie more than my mom does, don't you? My mom says she does –'

'I think Gracie's the most-loved kid on this mountain.'

'Clarence was loved and it didn't matter at all,' she says, sitting back against the couch cushion. 'The Drifter still got him.'

'Pilar?'

Her eyes close again. 'Hm?'

'I have something to tell you.'

'I have something to tell *you*,' Pilar says back, opening her eyes and blinking heavily. I don't know what to do. She's so scared. And I don't want to scare her more.

'I love you,' I tell her.

'I love you, too, Professor,' she says.

She sleeps like that, sitting straight up, facing me. The sun goes all the way down and I count the stones of the fireplace in the darkness. When the clock strikes five-thirty, I carefully get off the couch and go into the kitchen, lighting a candle so I won't wake Pilar. There's tofu thawing on the counter, a print-out of a recipe beside it.

'OK,' I say aloud. 'I can do this.'

By six o'clock I've impressed myself by cooking up a passable stir-fry. Grace woke up a few minutes ago, and has been sitting sleepily at the counter, eating the oat cereal I laid out for her, and colouring. Pilar's parents' car lights sweep across the room. I switch the kitchen light on and walk over to the couch.

'Hey, Pilar?' I say. 'My mom's coming soon. Do you want to get up?'

She gasps. 'I'm up.'

'OK.'

'Turn on the light,' she says. I do. Her house looks so much more alive in the light. She rubs her eyes, squeezing my hand. 'OK,' she says. 'OK.' She gets up. 'You cooked? Oh, Dylan, thank you.'

'Don't thank me yet,' I say. 'Taste it first.'

She walks over to the stove and takes a spoonful. 'It's good!' she says, adding about fifteen more herbs. 'Thank you,' she says.

'Are you all right?' I ask.

'Totally. I just needed sleep.'

A car horn beeps outside.

'That's my mom. Are you sure you're all right?'

'Yep,' she says. She hugs me lightly, and laughs. 'I slept away all my strength.'

In the driveway my mom and Pilar's parents are standing close together with crossed arms, talking. They stop when I come outside.

We all look like a bunch of zombies at school the next day. I can tell that nobody else is sleeping either. At lunch we eat mostly in silence. It takes me a while to realise everyone else at our table has stopped chewing. I look up and see MayBe and Thea are looking at Pilar. And Pilar is staring right at Cate.

'What's going on?' I ask.

Cate looks up from her pudding. 'What?'

'What the fuck,' Pilar says, standing up, 'is that?'

Cate looks behind her. 'What?'

'Where did you get that?' Pilar's voice is shaking.

'What?' Cate asks again, her voice faltering.

'What the hell is wrong with you?' Pilar yells, lunging over the table and grabbing at the zipper of Cate's sweatshirt. Pilar yanks it down, hard.

We recoil, all of us moving our chairs back away from Cate.

'Jesus, Cate,' MayBe says. 'Why would you *do* that?'

Cate pulls away from Pilar, zipping up her sweatshirt. It's too late, though. We all saw it.

Over her long-sleeved white sweatshirt is the green T-shirt we wore on the first anniversary of Clarence's death. She's cut down the sides of the collar to fit it over her head, and I'm guessing she cut off the sleeves, too. She must have taken it from the back of my photo album.

'Sick.' Thea hisses the word at Cate.

'Why would you do that, Cate? Why would you wear that?' MayBe is pleading.

'If I lived here,' Cate says finally, 'I would remember what today is.' Her chin is jutted out. She looks like a stubborn little kid.

Pilar looks at me. 'Did you give her that shirt?'

I shake my head. I still can't believe this is happening.

'Listen, princess,' Pilar spits, 'we're not in the habit of picking each other's scabs here. And even if we don't say out loud what day it is today, you bet we remember. We're the ones who were there. You need to quit your morbid fascination with this, little girl. You need to grow up and leave it alone.'

'Like you guys? Grow up and pretend it didn't happen? Eleven years ago *today*!'

Cate levels her gaze at me. It's too late for me to stand up and away from her reach when she grabs my collar and yanks it down, hard. With her other hand she reaches and digs her nails into the Band-Aid on my chest. She rips it off, leaving red half-moons from her nails.

Pilar grabs Cate's arm. 'What the hell are you doing?'

Cate doesn't answer, she just wrenches her arm free and shoves the Band-Aid in Pilar's face. The three photographs – Clarence, Tessa and Brian – are stuck to the edges. 'See, Dylan remembers. At least she has a heart. Not like the rest of you.'

She drops the Band-Aid on to the lunch table and walks away.

We all stay standing, staring at the wrinkled Band-Aid and bent pictures lying upside down on the lunch table.

MayBe finally reaches forward and picks up the small bundle. She hands it to me.

'Dylan,' Pilar says, 'what the hell is going on with you two?'

'I'm just . . .' I say.

'Do you guys have some sort of –' MayBe falters. 'Are

you guys making some sort of cult or something? Around the Drifter?'

'No!' I say. 'How could you ask that?'

'Because you're both freaking us out, dude!' Thea says loudly. 'God, what are you *doing*?'

I'm so tired. I sit back down at the lunch table.

'I'm lying to you,' I say, a sob working its way up my throat. 'I've always lied to you.'

'About what?' Pilar asks, sitting next to me.

I shake my head, crying harder. MayBe hands me a napkin.

'Don't make me tell you here,' I say, sobbing. 'I can't tell you.'

'After school, then,' Thea says sharply. 'You can tell us what the hell's been going on with you.'

'We'll take the bus to the village,' MayBe says.

Pilar nods in agreement, never taking her eyes off me.

But Pilar isn't there when we get on the bus. We ask Dottie to wait for her, and she does, but Pilar just doesn't come.

'Maybe she went home?' MayBe asks.

'Maybe she didn't care about your *big* secret,' Thea says. 'You still going to tell us?'

We're all squeezed into one seat, me sandwiched

239

between them. Thea snorts. 'You're not going to tell us, are you?'

'Where'd Cate go, anyway?' MayBe asks.

'She went home sick,' I answer. I saw her in the nurse's office, where I went for an aspirin after lunch.

'And where's Frank and Ben and Cray?' MayBe asks.

'Who knows,' Thea answers, a smirk flickering over her face.

We get off the bus in the village.

'Where to?' Thea asks. 'Where's the best place to tell a secret around here?'

'This way,' I say, and step into the narrow alley I use to get to the police station. I walk halfway down and stop.

MayBe bumps into me, and Thea into her.

'What, this is it?' Thea asks.

I nod, turning around to face them; the space is just barely wide enough.

'Very dramatic,' Thea says, crossing her arms.

'Thea, be nice,' MayBe says.

'So, what is it? What's your big lie?' Thea asks, smirking.

I look from MayBe to Thea, wishing Pilar were here. It'd be easier to say it to her, I think. I don't even know *how* to say it.

'I see . . . dead kids.'

Thea laughs. 'Like in that movie? The "I see dead people" movie?'

'I love that movie,' MayBe says. 'It's a classic.'

'So,' Thea says, 'where do you see these dead kids? And do they know they're dead? Or are they waiting for that creepy-looking psychic kid to let them in on the secret?'

Even MayBe's laughing a little now, and I can hear in both of their laughter how much they want what I'm saying to not be true. How much they want me to laugh with them, to tell them I'm joking, and that my big secret is actually that I'm adopted or that Cate's my long-lost sister.

'Remember when Clarence died,' I start, and their laughter fizzles, 'and I went to the nurse because I threw up?'

They both nod.

'I threw up because I had a . . .' I clear my throat. 'A vision. Of Clarence.'

'A vision?' MayBe asks, her face pale.

'What sort of vision?' Thea asks.

'I saw him lying in the snow. I saw where the Drifter had left him.'

'Bullshit,' Thea says, popping the word like bubble gum. 'You're as sick as your new friend.'

'Dylan, why are you saying this?' MayBe asks. 'Why would you say something like that?'

'He was lying in the snow, and he didn't have any boots, and he didn't have his glasses, and he didn't have his hat.'

'We know all of that,' Thea says. 'We saw it on the news.'

'Where was I the night they found that little girl Tessa's body in Salvation?'

'How the hell should I know?' Thea asks. 'Wow, you are one messed up puppy.'

'Where were you?' MayBe asks. 'You left school early.'

'I was there. With Deputy Pesquera. I left school because I'd had a –'

'A vision?' Thea asks with mock excitement.

'Yes.'

'So, what? You and Pesquera drove down to Salvation and helped them dig up that little girl?'

'Thea,' MayBe says softly.

'What? That's what she's saying. Right, Dylan? You go down there with a shovel and do some digging? *Or*,' she says, laughing and tapping her forehead, 'do you use your super *mind powers* to dig the hole?'

'You were in school the next day, though,' MayBe says.

242

'We got back late, after three a.m. I didn't want to stay home from school the next day.'

Thea stops laughing. 'Wait. What?'

'We got back in the middle of the night.'

She leans against the alley wall and studies her fingernails. 'You see anybody on your way?'

'Frank and Cray,' I say quickly, 'painting the Willows sign.'

Thea snorts. 'That doesn't prove anything.'

'Wait,' MayBe says. 'Is that how you knew about Clarence's house? About him dying there, not in the woods? Is that why you freaked out?'

'Yes.'

'Do you know who the Drifter is?' Thea asks.

'No.'

'Some psychic,' she scoffs. 'I don't believe you.'

'I know you don't.'

'What number am I thinking of?' she asks quickly, laughing.

'Five,' I answer.

'Lucky,' she says, laughing nervously.

'Four hundred and seventeen,' I say, stepping toward her.

She swallows a laugh.

'Thirty-nine.' I move closer. 'Fourteen, twenty-one, zero, zero, zero, stop thinking, stop thinking, stop thinking, stop thinking.'

My nose is almost touching hers now.

'Stop it,' Thea whispers. 'Please stop it.'

I step back.

'Was she right?' MayBe asks Thea. 'Did she guess right?'

'Is that why you made us sing that stupid song?' Thea asks.

'What song?'

'*Drifter, Drifter's coming for you*,' Thea sings in a little girl falsetto.

'We all sang that song,' I say quickly.

'Yeah, because you made us,' she says sharply. 'You always were a freaky kid.'

'It's true, Dylan,' MayBe says. 'You made up that song and made us sing it over and over and over again. It kind of creeped us all out.'

'Wha–' I shake my head, confused, thinking back to the summer under my back porch, making up the song . . . And then I remember. I lined them up, the three of them – Pilar, Thea, and MayBe against the wall under the porch. We'd just had popsicles and were chewing on the sticks, our lips orange and purple and green. I said, *You have to help me remember*. And then I taught them the song.

'So we helped you remember that stupid song,' Thea says. 'Now what?' She levels her eyes at me and sings, '*First snow's coming and he's coming back.*' She glances up as the first flakes of winter start to fall. When she looks back at me, she's gone pale. 'I used to think he controlled the weather,' she says, her eyes tearing. 'I thought he was the one who made it snow.'

'Does Cate know?' MayBe asks.

I tell them she does, and tell them how obsessed she's gotten, how I can't handle her questions any more, or the way she seems to almost wish she'd been here when Clarence died.

'I can't believe you told Cate and not Pilar,' MayBe says. 'I thought you and Pilar knew all each other's secrets.'

They both promise not to tell Pilar, agreeing that she should hear it all from me. We sit in silence outside of Mountain Candy, waiting for Thea's mom to come pick us up.

'It's pretty,' MayBe says, cautious about breaking the silence. We are looking out at the snow falling, the coloured lights, and the way-festive decorations that now have completely taken over the village. 'I love Christmas up here.'

'Me, too,' Thea and I both say at the same time. She gives me a nudge with her elbow and smiles. 'Jinx, buy me a Coke.'

'Next year we'll be seniors, so we get to ride on Santa's fire engine in the parade,' MayBe says, smiling.

'And peg little kids in the head with bubble gum and candy canes.' Thea laughs.

I laugh too.

'Dude,' Thea says, 'I can't believe you're a freaking psychic.'

'I know,' I groan. 'Weird, right?'

'Weird ain't the half of it,' Thea says, smiling at me. 'I'm glad you told us, Dylan.'

'Me too,' MayBe says. 'And there's Thea's mom.'

'They'll find him, you know,' Thea says as we stand, jutting her chin out. 'The Drifter's toast. Pesquera will track him down and shoot off his gunnysack if he so much as looks at this mountain again.'

'Sheriff Dean should have found him the first time,' I say. We're standing outside of the car; none of us has opened a door yet.

'He did his best, don't you think, though?' MayBe asks. 'He did all he could.'

'Dylan's right, it wasn't enough. Pesquera, though,'

Thea says. 'There's a lady you can hang your hope on.'
Thea's mom honks the horn.

'Will you call us after you tell Pilar?' MayBe asks,
opening the car door. 'So we know that we all know?'

'Sure I will,' I answer.

The radio is on in the car, but none of us sing. It's not
an angry ride home. The quiet is actually nice, with just
the radio and the sound of the windshield wipers to keep
it company.

Mom's sitting at the kitchen table drinking a cup of tea
when I get home. I get a mug of my own and use the
leftover hot water to make a cup of instant hot chocolate.
I sit across the table from her.

'How was school today?' she asks.

'Kind of . . . terrible.'

'How so?'

I shake my head. I don't know how much to tell her,
or where to start. I know she'll be mad at me for telling
Cate and now for telling my other friends, and then she'll
get mad again when I tell Pilar. I used to understand, but
not any more. I don't want to be ashamed any more. It's
not my fault. I decide to not tell her anything until I tell
Pilar. That way, she'll *have* to talk to me about

it. She can't make me hide it any more.

'I don't know,' I say. 'Pilar and I got in a fight.'

'You kids are under an awful lot of stress, with this whole Drifter mess,' Mom says. 'I don't think it's good for you.'

I laugh. I can't help it. 'You think? You think knowing that the crazed killer who murdered our friend is inching his way back up the mountain is *not* good for us?'

She sets down her teacup. 'That's exactly what I'm saying. What's gotten into you?'

'Nothing,' I answer. 'Nothing at all.'

We eat dinner in front of the TV and I think we're both glad to avoid conversation. I go up to my room early and try Pilar again. She didn't answer her cell phone before dinner, and even though I know it'll probably piss off her mom, I call on their house line this time.

'It's nine-thirty. Is this an emergency?'

'No, Mrs Alvarez. I'm just trying to reach Pilar. Is she in?'

'Pilar doesn't take calls after eight on school nights. Who is this?'

I know she knows it's me. They have caller ID. 'It's Dylan, Mrs Alvarez. How are you?'

'Fine. Dylan, please don't call this late again.'

'Will you please tell Pilar I called.'

'Yes. Good night.'

She hangs up before I can say another word.

I haven't talked to Cate since lunch today. I thought maybe she'd call me or show up at my house, but she hasn't. It feels like what happened today tore something between us, something that was stretched thin already – the sort of shell of a friendship we had, based only on her unending curiosity about Clarence, and about me.

14

I fall asleep quickly and am back in the desert. The same hole, the same barrel, the same footsteps behind me. I realise something. All those nights, all those nights of standing here, in this same spot, trying so hard to leave this place, to wake up to the safety of my room . . . That was what he wanted. I'm tired of running. This time I don't try to turn, I don't try to talk to whoever it is, and I just stand still. The footsteps get closer and closer. The hair on my arms and on the back of my neck raises, a feeling like cold water washes over my scalp and down my back, and I feel like if I don't move, if I don't scream, my heart will burst inside my chest. I grip my fists, digging my nails into my palms, and stay still. The footsteps pause for a moment, just out of my line of vision, and then continue. It's a man, his jeans and flannel shirt rustling and snapping in the breeze. He walks purposefully away from me, and then turns. I know his face. I *know* his face. But I can't for the life of me remember who he is.

I wake up but keep my eyes closed. There is something at the foot of my bed. The air in the room has gone cold. My dream has given me courage. I open my eyes.

I would like to say that I calmly greeted the ghost of my great-grandmother, but, my newfound courage gone, what I actually say is, 'Oh, sweet baby Jesus, don't kill me.'

She smiles at me, but does not move closer. She sits on the edge of the mattress, her hands folded in her lap. I can just see the halo of her hair, the strong shape of her shoulders, the straightness of her back.

'I want to turn on a light,' I whisper.

She nods, and I lean over and switch on the lamp by my bed, tucking my hands and body quickly back under the covers so just the tip of my nose and my eyes are sticking out.

She is smaller in the light. Her long grey hair is knotted at the nape of her neck, and I look quickly away from the familiar blue of her eyes and see the colour is echoed in the tiny blue flowers on her long dress, and the blue veins that press the surface of her wrinkled hands. She moves her head slightly, dipping it into my line of vision and catching my eyes with hers. She straightens back up, pulling my own head straight and out from under the covers with her gaze, until we are both sitting straight, staring at each other.

'I look like you,' I say.

She nods again.

'We have the same chin, and nose . . .'

Can ghosts talk? I'm almost afraid to find out. What if I ask her a question and she opens her mouth and bats fly out of it?

'And our eyes are the same, but I think I might be taller than you. My dad was tall . . .'

When she finally opens her mouth, I duck under my covers, almost feeling the soft punches of a million bat wings beating against the blankets. There are two sounds when she speaks. The dry, creaking groan of her words, and a smoother sound like river water over rocks.

'You need to ask your mama about that pickle jar,' she says, a slow tremor of impatience making it sound like she's been pushing me to do this for years.

I peek out from under the covers. No bats. Just my great-grandmother, watching me.

'Wha . . . what?'

'Ask her,' she urges, more kindly.

All of the questions I've ever wanted to ask crash into one another in my brain. All I can come up with is, 'Does it hurt to be dead?'

She doesn't answer, but leans toward me, making me

cry out when, with a flicker, she appears sitting right next to my head. My great-grandmother reaches toward me and rests her hands on either side of my face, the conclusion of the movement she started so many years ago in the nursing home before she died.

'How'd that song go?' she asks in her two-tone voice, and then she disappears.

I *sleep* all night. Dreamless and perfect sleep.

When I wake up, rested for the first time in a long time, I can tell from the hush outside that it has snowed hard during the night. I walk across the cold floor and look outside, happy to see the trees caked with thick bunches of snow.

Mom is downstairs in the kitchen, chopping vegetables.

'I thought I'd make you an omelette before school. You've had enough Chocolate-O's lately. You need a hot breakfast. Did you see the snow?' she asks, smiling.

I sit down at the kitchen table. 'I saw Great-grand-mama last night.'

Mom stops her chopping for a minute, shakes her head, and starts chopping again. 'Well, I guess you would.' I tip my head to see the side of Mom's face, to make sure she's the one who's talking. Because it's not her voice coming out of her mouth; instead it's a drawl, warm and

253

slow and teasing, spoken gravelly from the little hollow at the base of her throat. Goose bumps ripple their way up and down my arms and across the back of my neck.

'What'd she say?' Mom asks, the unfamiliar smoothness of her words nearly hiding a sharp edge under their surface. 'Come on, now,' she teases. 'Grandmama never was one to keep thoughts to herself. Hers or anybody else's.'

'She said to ask you about the pickle jar.'

Even Mom's laugh is different, her mouth wide, her head tipped back, her eyes closed. I wonder now, watching her, if she's ever been happy before right now. 'That old bag never could let a thing rest.'

'Mom? Why are you talking like that?'

'Because, darling, this is how we'd reel 'em in; voices like sugar syrup warmed up by the sun.'

'Mom . . .' I'm pleading.

She clucks and then turns to smile at me. 'It's me, baby. You just never really heard my voice, is all.' And it's true. This voice, this unfamiliar slowed-down voice that lilts and curls and takes a nap midword, sounds more like my mom than her almost careful-sounding mountain accent.

'Yes, I have,' I say, a memory tickling at me.

'You *do* remember,' Mom says, smiling. 'They

wanted you, you know. They wanted me to leave you there when Grandmama died. Well, they said they wanted me to stay too, but I didn't believe them. It was you they wanted.'

I remember then, my mom holding me in a crowded wood-panelled room. I was too old to be held and I kept squirming to get down. It was the funeral, I realise now, the funeral for Great-grandmama. There were hands reaching for me, a woman with eyes just like my mom's, a woman who smiled at me and said, *Come here, child*. My mom held on too tight, made me cry out. *You can't have her*, my mom said. *She's not like you*. And the woman with my mom's eyes laughed and said, *Bull crackers*. *That child's as touched as the day is long*.

'You want me to tell you a story?' Mom asks, wiping her hands on a dish rag and sitting down next to me.

I nod.

'Let's have us a story, then,' she says. We make tea first, or tea for Mom and hot chocolate for me. We go into the living room and sit down on the couch. For once the television isn't on.

'Our house wasn't in town,' Mom starts. 'That was the first thing. It was miles from anywhere worth going. Some people didn't trust us. Females, living out there alone. A lot of people didn't think it was right, or proper, all of us women with no men around. Especially with the way things were at our house.' Mom laughs. 'I swear to you, it was a house full of people plumb out of their minds. Your aunts Ruby and Peg, my mom, my grandma – all of them. Crazy people.'

'What was so crazy about them?'

'Oh,' she says, sounding annoyed, 'they all had . . . notions. Lies, mostly. Maybe some of it was true. I never could tell, and that's what drove me so crazy. It wasn't unusual at our house to sit at the breakfast table and hear everyone but me talk about someone that they'd visited while they slept. No, darling, you are not the only one who gets dead people creaking the floorboards in the middle of the night. My sisters would come downstairs with stories about Granddad said this or Great-Aunt Rhonda said that.'

'You didn't believe them?' I ask.

'Sometimes,' she says. 'Sometimes not. That was the problem. I never could tell when they were lying or putting me through the wringer for being the only one who had some sense in that house, the only normal one, the only one who wasn't . . .'

'Wasn't what?'

Mom sighs. 'I was embarrassed by my mother, Dylan, by our rickety old house, and by my sisters. We had multi-coloured Christmas lights strung up on our porch all year round, and a dozen wind chimes, made out of wood or silverware or glass or anything else we could find lying around the house that would clack and clunk and ting and ping, but they never *chimed*. I wanted wind chimes that made a delicate tinkling sound when the wind blew. I didn't want a chorus of broken sounds coming from broken objects strung up together and hung wherever you could hammer a nail to hang them on.

'Our front porch was screened in and half-sunk into the ground, but that's where we spent most of our time, especially in the summer, because the fan on the ceiling kept things tolerably cool. There was a white wicker couch out there with a faded rose-pattern cushion, and a few other chairs that didn't even match each other. That's where we would do it.'

'Do what?'

'That's where,' Mom says, leaning closer to me, her eyes wide, her voice dropped to a whisper, 'we would tell the *future*.'

My jaw drops. 'You . . . You know how to do that?'

'Me?' Mom says, laughing. 'Not me. I could do

numbers, but that was ninety-nine per cent horse crap. It didn't take any real –'

'Numbers?'

'Numbers. Think of a number between one and ten.'

I think of the number nine.

'Now picture what it looks like when you write it.'

I do, picturing a thick black marker on a piece of white paper.

'Now look, in your mind, at the number you just wrote.'

Mom settles back on the couch, and commences staring at me. Her eyes holding on to mine, not letting me look away. The expression on her face doesn't change, it keeps the same intensity for a full minute.

'Seven,' she says.

I laugh. 'Wrong!'

'Really?' she asks, the same calm expression on her face.

'Well, yeah. I guessed number nine.'

'Did you?' she asks.

'Yep!'

'Are you sure about that?'

I was until she asked me that question. I did pick nine, right? I try to remember the number I drew, the thick black line, but now all I can see is a drawing of the number seven.

'How'd you do that?'

'Made you doubt yourself,' she says, laughing. 'Pay me a quarter and I'll tell you how old you'll be when you marry and how many babies you're going to have. And then by the time you find out if I'm right or not, I'll be so far gone from this one-horse town, people will barely remember my name.'

I study my cup of hot chocolate.

She touches my shoulder. 'You can do numbers, can't you?' she asks.

'Fifteen,' I say, looking at her.

She laughs so hard I almost spill my hot chocolate. 'Your aunt Ruby is going to *love* that! She does numbers too, among other things.'

'Why's she calling so much lately?'

'Because she's damned psychic, that's why. You ever notice how she calls only when I'm not home? She knows she's not supposed to do that, but she does it anyway. I made her swear she wouldn't tell you about our crazy family.'

'She didn't.'

'Good.'

'So . . . tell me about my crazy family.'

'They looked ridiculous, first of all. Ruby and Peg. Flimsy dresses, wearing two or three at a time, and strings of beads and heavy rings they'd pull from Grandmama's jewellery box. It was like Halloween every day with them. And our mama wasn't much better. She'd wear these high-collared black dresses that went down to the floor, and pull her hair up on top of her head, and she'd just look really *severe*, like this.' Mom narrows her eyes at me. 'You remember, from the hospital.'

I nod.

'And Grandmama. Well, she just wore Granddad's old clothing. His boots, his pants, his button-up shirts, his hats. She looked ridiculous, just like the rest of them. I guess it worked, though. It brought people in.'

'In to what? Mom, I don't understand.'

'People would come see us and sit on our front porch, and they would ask us to tell them their future. And we would. Or at least Ruby and Peg would. Like I said, I just did numbers and made up future husbands for the little girls. Ruby and Peg did the serious stuff. Ruby especially. Everyone, except for me, could tell when somebody climbed up our porch steps with bad news coming. Peg hated giving people bad news. Ruby would do it, though, even though we all told her it was OK to lie about some things. She would tell anybody anything. She'd sit cross-legged on the wicker couch on the porch and pull the giant hairball of a porch cat on to her lap. She'd narrow her eyes at whoever was sitting across from her, and she'd tell them.'

'Tell them what?'

'Tell them everything. That their sons weren't coming home from war. That their wife was cheating on them. That there was poison in their blood and that's why their babies kept dying. Sometimes, if Grandmama saw somebody coming up on the porch before Ruby, and if Grandmama could tell just by looking at that somebody that Ruby would have a chance to tell some real bad news, she'd make Ruby go inside and she'd go out on the porch herself. And then she'd lie to whoever it was, and send them on their way. She said the people would find out themselves, and it was better just to tell them they'd be lucky in love with a house full of babies, and send them on their way. The pickle jar got filled, either way.'

'The pickle jar!' I say excitedly. 'That's what she meant.'

'Yes, that's what she meant.' Mom laughs. 'There's more to that story, though. I tried, for a long time, to be like my sisters. To be like my mom and my grandma. I would come downstairs and announce that Granddad had come to visit *me* in the night, that he had told *me* where he'd hid stashes of money before he died, just like he did to my sisters. When my sisters would tell your great-grandmama to look in his old hair oil container, or the toe of the right-footed wool slipper that had lost its left a long time ago, there would always be a neat roll of bills, dusty and bent from being stored so long. But when I would tell Grandma to look in the broken sugar bowl in the shed, or in his favourite jazz record album sleeve, she would just find the quarters that I'd taken from the pickle jar and stashed there myself. After a while, I realised that I was the normal one, not them. And I wanted a normal life. I wanted to wear neatly pressed slacks and eat real meals, not breakfasts of lemon candies and pretzels, because that's what some broke joker had paid us with the night before. I wanted a proper life, and that's why when your dad came through town –'

'My dad?'

'He was a college boy on a cross-country trip. He had all of this camera equipment in the back of his car and had come to take our pictures. He said he'd heard about us three counties over. I fell in love with him right off. And he – I think he fell in love with my family more than he did with me. But his clunky old station wagon stayed parked at our house for that whole summer, and in the fall we were married. And then in the spring . . .'

Mom touches my nose. 'We had you.'

'And then you left.'

Mom laughs. 'We sold his car and bought bus tickets and . . .' She sighs. 'We stole the money from that week's pickle jar. Which is why *my* mom still won't talk to me. I sent her the money back as soon as we got here, but she said it wasn't the same. I felt like she never really loved me like she did my sisters. All I ever wanted was for her to put her hands on my face' – Mom lays her cool palms against my cheeks – 'and tell me, "You've got the sight, girl, you have it strong." Like she did with my sisters.'

She stops talking, but doesn't move her hands. 'You've got the sight, girl,' she says, smiling at me. 'And I'm sorry I ever made you think it was something less than wonderful.'

I half-expect Cate to be waiting for me at the bottom of my driveway, but there is only Dottie idling the bus in the snow. She's been doing that lately, waiting for me, I think because the Drifter came back. I appreciate it.

Ben doesn't get on the bus, but his mom is there with JJ and Tye, wearing snow boots and a bathrobe. She motions to me to open my window.

'Tell Benji to call me when you see him, OK?' she asks.

'Sure,' I say.

'He stayed at Frank's last night, and he was supposed to call to check in, but he didn't.'

'I'll tell him to call.'

She waves at the boys and then walks back down the driveway.

15

I forget my math book in my locker after homeroom and go back for it. The halls are empty, just like homeroom was. The only people there were Thea, MayBe, and me. I'm shutting my locker and walking to class, when I see Ben leaning against the science lab door. He looks like he slept in his clothes, and his usually friendly face looks drawn and grey.

Ben looks away from me when I walk up to him.

'What's up?' I ask.

'Nothing,' he says, still avoiding my eyes.

'You making moonshine in there?' I try to see past him, through the window into the classroom.

'Go to class, Dylan,' he says stiffly.

'What's going on?' I ask, the hairs starting to stand up on the back of my neck.

'Go to class, Dylan,' he says again. He almost growls it.

'Why?'

Ben looks hard at me. 'Because we don't trust you any more.'

'What are you talking about?'

I try to see again into the empty classroom. Now I can see the lights are off and that someone is hunched in a chair, facing the back wall.

'Who is that?' I ask, pushing Ben out of the way and opening the door.

'Dylan, I'm handling this,' Ben says. He steps into the classroom behind me and shuts the door. It takes a second for my eyes to adjust to the light; there is a charred, acrid smell to the air.

The person in the back row is slumped so far he is almost falling forward and out of the chair. I walk closer and see his arms are limp by his sides, his fingers lightly brushing the floor.

'Frank?' I say, stepping in front of him and touching his shoulder. He doesn't move.

'Ben, what's wrong with Frank?'

He doesn't answer me, just looks nervously to the door.

I kneel down next to Frank, my nose stinging from the acrid stench wafting off him. 'You guys go camping?'

'Frank!' I say louder, shaking him, 'Frank!' It's then I see his neck, the charred and blistered skin spreading up under his chin.

I jump back and grab Ben's arm. 'What did you do?'

Ben pulls away. 'I'm handling this, Dylan.'

'Handling what? What the hell did you guys do?'

For a second Ben looks completely helpless. '*We* didn't do anything,' he says, 'because they didn't call me. I waited for them in the barn, all night. And Cray didn't call until this morning, and then it was too late.'

'Where's Cray?'

'He took off after he called me.'

'What did they *do*, Ben?'

'They burned it,' he says, looking at Frank. 'At least they tried to.'

'Burned what?'

'The Willows,' Deputy Pesquera says, walking quickly through the door and turning on the lights. We all flinch at its brightness, all of us, except for Frank. His burn looks even worse in the light, and I can see his shirt melted to his skin, the burn extending down to his left hand.

'Dylan, go to the office and get the principal and the nurse. Ben, stay right here where I can see you.'

'Is he dead?' I ask, faltering by the door.

'Not yet,' the deputy says. 'Go.'

Ben and I wait in the back of the deputy's truck while they load Frank into the ambulance. I've never ridden in the back before. Ben won't talk to me. He just keeps staring out the window. He's shaking. So am I.

The sight comes suddenly, piercing my vision, tearing it in half, until I am seeing a little red snow boot, half-buried in the snow.

'She's freaking out,' I hear Ben say when the front door to the truck opens. I feel his hands on my back, my own hands pressing against my eyes. 'Jesus, what's wrong with her!'

The vision leaves as suddenly as it came, and I am looking at the red-black colour made by pressing my hands against my eyes. I am leaning back against the seat, and Ben is whispering, 'Dylan, are you all right?'

I shake my head. 'Deputy . . .'

'We're on our way,' she says.

I cradle my head in my hands, the rocking of the truck making it feel like my skull is going to splinter into pieces. Ben keeps his hand on my back, rubbing small circles. I shake my head when he asks me what's wrong.

We go up the side entrance to the police station, and Lucy looks at us in surprise. 'Dylan?'

Deputy Pesquera raises her hand to silence Lucy, and hustles Ben and me through the reception door.

'Deputy,' I hear Lucy say behind us. 'We have a problem.'

Pilar is there, standing in the hall outside of Deputy Pesquera's office. Sheriff Dean is beside her, saying something in a low voice. I don't know why I run to her, why I don't wonder first what she's doing here.

'Pilar,' I say, grabbing her arms. 'Pilar, I want to tell you my secret.' I stare into her face, tears streaming down my own. 'I see things, Pilar. I see little kids when they've died. I see them in my head. That's my secret, Pilar. I saw Clarence, and the little girl Tessa from Salvation, and the little boy Brian from down the hill, I saw them all, Pilar, I saw them when they were dying. I only see them when they're dying. I never find them alive, and that's why I never told you, because it's awful, Pilar, it's so ugly and I thought you'd stop loving me and . . .' I gulp. 'I see a girl, Pilar. I see her in my head. I know she's dying. I know that's why I'm seeing her. I know that's why I'm here, to help them find her . . .' I stop talking.

Pilar sways a little and I think she might fall. And then she opens up her mouth and screams. And screams. And screams. I look around wildly to see Sheriff Dean, the familiar beige of a file folder in his hand, reaching out toward Pilar. The picture on the front of the folder. It's Grace.

Pilar slaps me, hard across the cheek, whipping my head to the side. I see Ben, staring in confusion, and the deputy rushing toward us.

Sheriff Dean pulls Pilar back, trying to move her into his office.

'Pilar!' I cry. 'Please!'

Pilar pulls away from the sheriff and grabs my shoulders. 'Tell me where she is.' She shakes me, my head whipping back and forth. 'Tell me where she is!' she screams into my face, shaking me again. 'Where is my Gracie!'

They separate us. Me in Deputy Pesquera's office, Pilar down the hall in Sheriff Dean's, waiting for her parents to come up the hill, and Ben in the interview room.

Deputy Pesquera sits at her desk.

'Can't I at least look at the picture?' I ask. My tears are gone. I feel dried out, a husk.

The deputy shakes her head. 'Sheriff Dean wants to wait on that.'

'Why's he the sheriff again all of a sudden? He's never around any more.'

'He never stopped being sheriff, Dylan. He's just holding off retiring until we catch the Drifter.'

'So he can take the credit?'

'So he can sleep at night.'

'So you think it's the Drifter?' I ask. 'You think he has Grace?'

'We don't know yet.'

'Then why are we sitting here? Why aren't we out looking for her?'

'We've got the volunteer deputies –'

I laugh. 'Great. That's just perfect. Volunteer deputies clomping around in the first snow . . .' The end of the sentence gets lost somewhere between my brain and my tongue. *How'd that song go?* I remember my great-grandmother's question from last night.

'You all right?' the deputy asks.

'You ever search his house?' I ask. 'Clarence's?'

'Of course we did. Why?'

'He died there, you know.'

She studies me. 'Yes, I know that. How do *you* know that?'

'You can't hide under the bed,' I chant. *'He'll find you and crack your head.'*

The song loops in my mind, and then I'm there, standing in the doorway of Clarence's bedroom. The mural on his wall is fresh and new, his toys are neatly stacked in one side of his toy box. On the empty side is a piece of

271

notebook paper with the words 'Your Side' carefully written in crayon. His closet is the same way, his clothes all pushed to one side, leaving half of the rack empty. A piece of paper hangs taped to the clothing rod. *Your Side*, it says. There is a collapsible cot against the mural wall, and Clarence is carrying his teddy bear from his bed to the cot, and laying it carefully on the pillow. 'Yours,' he says aloud. He is halfway dressed for school, wearing corduroys but no shoes or socks, an undershirt but no sweater. He looks out of the window, and at first I think he's waving to the falling snow. Then I see the man in the window, pulling it open and crawling through. Clarence knows him; he claps his hands and laughs. 'You silly! You're supposed to use the door!' And then I am Clarence, and the man is squeezing, squeezing my shoulders, and I am squirming out of his grip and I am crawling under the bed and he is pulling me out by my foot and I am looking up at the man's head, hallowed by the overhead light, his red, red hair looking like it's on fire, his thick sunglasses blackening his eyes like a raccoon, just like the ones he wore in the picture on Cate's refrigerator.

'Oh, shit,' I whisper. *You'll see his face in someone else. And she won't know, even herself.* The shavings would stick to his boots on the days he 'walked the floor'. I am out of that room, and back in this one, lying on the grimy floor in front of the deputy's desk, looking up at the peeling tiles in the ceiling. The deputy is bending over me, and I blink away her fingers lifting at my lids.

'Can you sit up?' she asks.

'The shavings – I know who left them,' I say, pulling myself back up into the chair. 'You have to take me. You have to take me with you.'

'What –'

'I know where she is!' I shout, standing with shaking legs. 'You have to take me with you! I can show you where she is!'

'I'll take you,' the deputy says.

'Not without her,' I say. 'Not without Pilar.'

The Croondon houses stand at attention as the deputy pulls her truck into the cul-de-sac. Pilar and I sit in the back. She hasn't said a word to me. In the blank house faces I see judgement, I see *We've been waiting for you.*

'Here?' the deputy asks.

I nod.

'Stay in the truck,' Deputy Pesquera says, opening her door. At the same time, the cracked and peeling door to Clarence's old house opens. 'Stay in the truck!' the deputy says again, getting out of the truck and slamming the door behind her, lifting her walkie-talkie to her mouth as she does.

The door to Clarence's house stays halfway open, whoever's inside blacked out by the shadow of the door.

'Is she dead?' Pilar asks.

I start to say *I'm sorry*, but I'm interrupted by Pilar screaming and lunging over me, opening the door and falling out of the truck and jumping up into a run. I get out after her and look to Clarence's house, and see Grace standing on the doorstep in her red winter boots, stomping her feet and holding up her hands. Deputy Pesquera is running toward her, but Pilar streaks by her with a yell. I run too, but stop dead when Grace squeals 'Mommy!' as Pilar swings her up and against her chest.

'I'm here,' Pilar says, burying her face into Grace's neck, her voice ragged with tears. 'Mommy's here.'

'Oh my God,' I whisper.

There is laughter from the front door, a hardened, crass version of a familiar giggle.

'Cate?'

She steps out of the house and on to the front steps, and even though she's still laughing, her face looks like she's seen a ghost.

'Worst! Psychic! Ever!' She cackles, pointing at me,

and then at Pilar, who has carried Grace back to the deputy's truck. 'You didn't know?' Cate asks, still pointing, her hand shaking. 'You didn't know about *that*? God, even *I* guessed that!'

'Cate? That's your name, right?' Deputy Pesquera says, moving toward her.

'Wait!' Cate says, pointing now at the deputy. 'Just wait, please.'

'OK,' the deputy says, raising her hands. 'Just tell me why we're waiting and we'll wait.'

Cate drops her arm to her side and looks at me, her pale face pulled down into a terrible look of heartbreak. 'Did you know?' she asks, shrugging.

'Know what?' I ask.

'I wasn't supposed to come here today,' she says. 'I was supposed to go to school. I was going to apologise to you, and to Thea, and to Pilar, and to MayBe.' She screams at me. 'I was going to tell you the truth!'

'So tell me the truth, Cate,' I say softly, stepping toward her.

'Stop!' she says, raising her hands. She glares at the deputy, who has moved closer. 'Both of you. Please stop.' She starts to cry. 'Just please stop and let me figure this . . . I was afraid you wouldn't forgive me for what I've done.'

275

'What have you done, Cate?' I ask, not needing the deputy's nod to encourage me to keep Cate talking.

'I've lied to you,' she says, sobbing. 'I've always lied to you.'

She hangs her head, crying for a moment, and then she looks up suddenly. 'Why is she here?' she asks, looking over my shoulder, to where Pilar and Grace are. 'Why was that little girl in Clarence's room?' She looks behind her, into the house. 'I didn't think anyone would be here, but I found her, and I was going to call the police, but then you . . .' She stares at me, her mouth going slack. 'How did you know she was here?'

'I saw her.'

'But . . .' Cate says, her face wrinkling like a child's, 'you said you only saw dead kids, you never saw them alive. I always asked you and you always said you only saw them –'

'I know, but you were right!' I say, walking toward her. 'You were so right, Cate. I was only afraid. I was afraid of what I'd see if I let myself. But I *saw* Grace. I saw her and she was still alive. You were right, Cate, you were right all along.'

Cate recoils, stepping back a little into the house, her face shadowed by the darkness indoors until she sticks her face back out into the light and splits me in half with her scream. 'Then, why couldn't you save my little brother?'

My knees give out beneath me and I drop to the ground. 'No, no, no,' I moan, reaching out my hands to her, understanding everything now.

'Why couldn't you save Clarence!' she screams. 'I was supposed to come and live here! We were supposed to be a family again! You ruined everything!'

'I didn't know, Cate,' I cry. 'I didn't know.'

'We were going to share a room and go to kindergarten together! He was going to give me half his toy box, and half his closet, and he was going to introduce me to all his friends! Mom and Dad were going to get back together and everything was going to be perfect!'

'I'm sorry,' I cry, hiding my face in my hands. 'I'm so sorry.'

'You stole my life!' I look up, and she is standing in front of me. She drops to her knees. 'Don't you see?' she says, taking my hands and squeezing them too hard. 'I was supposed to be in all those class pictures with you. I was supposed to make snow-angels with you and help teach MayBe how to say her R and make five dollars an hour sweeping up at Thea's mom's salon. But none of that happened.' Her tears are gone. Now there is only quiet fury. 'Because you are a coward. You could have saved that little girl in the desert and that boy down the hill and all those kids in between, but you didn't because you're too much of a goddamn coward to really ever see what you're capable of.' She looks behind me. 'Dad?'

I recognise Cate's father's car as it comes racing up the driveway, spinning out as he slams on the brakes and tries to turn around and drive back down. Sheriff Dean blocks his way, pulling the police cruiser sideways and jumping out of the car with his gun drawn. Deputy Pesquera covers Cate's eyes.

You'll see his face in someone else
And she won't know, even herself.

16

Pilar and I walk in silence through the snow, which is finally deep enough for us to have traded in our high-tops for real snow boots. We follow the path from the village down to the frozen lake, the sounds of laughter, ice skates, and sleds meeting us halfway. With the first snow being so late, it took a long time for the lake to freeze this year. Now, though, in the ice cold of January, it has finally turned solid.

I keep stealing glances at Pilar, seeing how her face has changed over the past several weeks. She looks rested, the dark circles under her eyes are gone, and her face is fuller and doesn't have the squinched-up look I was starting to get used to.

'I didn't think you'd ever call,' I finally say.

'I wasn't sure I would either,' she answers. 'I was pretty mad at you. I still am, sometimes.'

I nod.

'My parents have been homeschooling me,' she

says. 'But I guess you would have heard that.'

'My mom told me. How is that going?'

'It's . . . fine. They're pretty heavy on the insect education though. I'm going back to school after January vacation. They just wanted me to stay out till things . . .' She hesitates. 'Blew over.'

'We miss you,' I tell her. 'Me and MayBe and Thea. Ben, too.'

'How is he doing without Frank and Cray?'

'He seems all right. He's halfway done with his community service. I help him with the horses a lot. I think he's pretty lonely.'

Pilar raises her eyebrows at me. It's such a relief to see her smile. 'He's *lonely*?'

'Please,' I laugh. 'I'd rather make out with Marge the Wonder Pony.'

'What about Frank? And Cray?'

'Both being tried as adults for arson.'

'Jesus. How's Thea?'

'A mess sometimes, but most of the time she's OK. She was supposed to be there that night, but Cray lied to her and gave her a bogus meeting place. He did the same thing to Ben. I guess, according to Cray, he was going to try to talk Frank out of it.'

'Do you think that's true?'

'I don't know. I'd like to think it is.'

'Who knew that new plastic crap they're building the Willows out of isn't flammable.'

'Not Frank.'

'No, definitely not Frank.' She snorts. 'And what about *her?*'

I know who she's talking about. 'She's back east, with relatives. They're trying to figure out if she is going to have to testify against her dad or not.'

'Do you miss her?'

Her question catches me off guard.

'I mean,' she says, not hiding the thread of hurt in her voice, 'you guys were pretty close.'

I can't even manage to shrug, caught up in the memory of how Cate's body felt when it went limp against me. I'd pulled her into a hug when Sheriff Dean ordered her father to the ground and then pressed his boot into her dad's neck. I told her not to look, but she did anyway and screamed for Sheriff Dean to stop. She shook and screamed *What's happening?* again and again. When she whispered in my ear, I think it was because she couldn't scream any more. She whispered, sobbing, *It was my dad, wasn't it?*

'She writes to me,' I finally say. 'Long letters.'

'Have you written her back?'

'A couple times. She called me a couple times.'

Pilar's face wrinkles. 'What'd she say?'

'Not much. She sounds kind of out of it. I think they might have medicated her or something. She wanted to talk about Clarence.'

Pilar snorts. 'Of course she did.'

'Not like that,' I say gently. 'She wanted to tell me about him.'

'Like what? What'd she tell you?'

I tell Pilar about the conversation, about how Cate kept saying that she'd send me the picture of her and Clarence in their playpen. She said they were fraternal twins, but if you saw the picture, you'd swear they were identical. She said they would crack each other up, sitting in the playpen together, gurgling jokes that nobody else understood.

'She remembered all that?' Pilar asks.

'I think a lot of it is what her mom told her.'

'What I don't get, though, is why didn't he . . .' She lets the question trail off.

'Kill Cate?' I ask.

'Well . . . yeah. I mean, it's not like he just went after

boys. And it's not like the fact that she's his daughter would have stopped him. Just look what he did to Clarence. And did her mom know? And if he was up here, why didn't her dad's DNA get tested?'

'Cate thinks . . .'

'Wait, you *asked* her about it?' Pilar says, touching my arm in surprise.

I look away from her and watch my boots slide into the deep snow. Step, step, step.

'We talked about a lot of things,' I finally say, letting my eyes meet Pilar's. She nods. 'Cate and Clarence's mom and dad were getting divorced, but according to Cate, things were still kind of friendly between them. Their mom moved out here to be with her sisters, to live with other Croondons. She took Clarence with her but left Cate with her dad, and the plan was that eventually Cate and her dad would move out here too. Cate would live with Clarence and her mom, and her dad would live somewhere else on the mountain and get to see the kids on weekends or something. The day that Clarence got killed was the day before Cate and her dad were supposed to come for a visit, to look for an apartment for her dad. Cate says they came the night before without telling anybody, checked into a hotel room down the hill, and then her dad left her in the room by herself on the morning Clarence got killed. She says when he got back to the room, they went to the airport and flew all the way back home. Nobody ever knew they'd come in the first place.'

'And she never told anybody?' Pilar asks angrily. 'She never thought that maybe that was a piece of important information?'

I shake my head. 'She thinks maybe she just blocked the whole thing out. The whole trip took less than twenty-four hours, and she was asleep for a lot of it. She thinks maybe he gave her something, to make her sleep, to make her groggy. Her dad acted like the trip never happened, so she did too.'

'But that still doesn't explain why he didn't just kill her too. Sorry if that's harsh, but I just don't get it.'

'She doesn't either. She thinks maybe whatever it was that made him kill Clarence went to sleep, into some sort of hibernation, when they got back east. She sounds like a little kid when she's talking about it. It's sad.'

'I guess,' Pilar says.

'Her mom went into a hospital close to where Cate and her dad lived, and the rest of the Croondons settled a few hours away. They were all from that area to begin with. She and her dad weren't really moving here, you know.'

Pilar looks at me in surprise.

'The family elected her dad to come out and take care of selling off the land to developers, the same people who built the Willows. It was only going to take a month or so, and Cate begged him to let her come too. She says when she came back here, the thing inside of him – the monster – woke up.'

Pilar shakes her head and we walk in silence for a while more. 'I heard her mom was, like, catatonic? In a hospital or something.'

'She's in a hospital, but she's aware of what's going on. The aunt that Cate's staying with lives close to the hospital, and Cate's gone to see her mom a couple times. She says her mom will only talk for a couple minutes, usually about Cate and Clarence in the playpen.'

Pilar shakes her head. 'You think Cate's mom knew? About her dad?'

'I don't know,' I say, slowly answering the question I've asked myself a million times. 'I think maybe when Clarence died something got severed in her brain. So maybe even if she knew, she didn't know she knew, you know?'

Pilar feigns confusion at my explanation, and then says, 'Yeah, I know.'

I pull a faded photograph from my pocket and hand it to Pilar.

'God, they do look alike,' she says, staring at Cate's and Clarence's slobbery and laughing faces, their pudgy baby hands gripping the side of the playpen. 'Do you think she really remembers Clarence at all?'

'I hope so.'

'Me too,' Pilar says, handing me back the picture. 'Her poor mom. I can't even imagine what that must have felt like. To lose your baby like that.'

Something catches in my throat, and I blurt out the first thing that comes into my head. 'You're a *mom*!' I don't mean it to sound accusing, but it does.

She sighs. 'I know.'

Neither of us says anything for a long while; we just keep clomping through the snow.

I make a squeaking sound in my throat, trying to keep my words inside. Pilar looks at me.

'Well, it's just *weird*!' I finally say, trying to keep my voice low. 'I mean, you pushed a whole human body through your hooha! AND you had sex!'

Pilar stifles a sigh, waiting for me to finish.

'Not necessarily in that order,' I mumble.

'I . . .' Pilar says.

'You didn't tell me!' I'm yelling now. 'How could you not tell me that, Professor? That's, like, the most major thing that's ever happened to you, and you didn't even tell me about it! You just let me go on . . . like a stupid idiot, like a stupid idiot kid while you had this major grown-up experience! Didn't you trust me? Didn't you trust me enough to tell me?'

I feel so far away from her, even standing right here, yelling in her face. It's like a thick clear wall of goo has come between us, like we'll never truly be together again.

Pilar says calmly, 'Remember when I first got to Montana, that summer I went away with my parents? I e-mailed you when I first got there and said there were no cute boys.'

I nod, the hot pulsing of my heartbeat slowing down as she talks.

'Well, Nate came a week later,' she says with a shy grin. 'And I full-on swooned over him. The way he wore a T-shirt and his cowboy hat, the way he cracked his knuckles, the way he stretched his back so that you could see the trail of hair on his belly under his T-shirt, the way he said "All *right*" when something was good. He's in the same grade as us. He grew up close to the university and volunteered to be the climbing instructor for my dad's class, show the students how to climb up trees to get samples.

'You would have died, Dylan, the way I flirted with this guy. I just . . . When he was around, I didn't even feel like myself. I felt better than myself. Braver. And –' she pauses, like she still can't believe it – 'he would flirt back! We started eating lunch together, and then we started going on walks together after class, and – God, my parents teased me about it nonstop. At that point they still thought it was cute. Nothing had really happened, we hadn't held hands or kissed, I could barely even look him in the eye. So then he asked me if I wanted to go on a hike one Saturday. I mean, that would have been enough for me to, like, live on for months, the fact that we were hiking together. But when we got to the waterfall and sat down on a rock, I had this *hope, hope, hope* that something would happen. And we sat there and he said, "I don't want to mess this up." I didn't say anything back, and he said, "I like you. I think about you all the time. I like your family. I like everything about you." And then he *asked* if he could kiss me.'

'And?'

'I kissed him and . . . You know the way you described the first time you and Ben kissed?'

'We were nine.'

'Well, yeah, but you said it was like you had fireworks going off in your heart.'

'I said that?' I laugh. 'Jeesh, I was a corny kid.'

'You were right, though, because that's what it felt like.'

'Wow.'

'And we started dating. I mean, he asked my parents first. Called them ma'am and sir. And they liked him, a lot. And I liked him –' her voice breaks – 'so much. When he was around, I would pray for a chance to touch him, for him to touch me. By the third month, the end of the summer, we were pretty –'

'Hot and heavy?'

She laughs. 'Exactly. And we were getting more and more serious and it sort of morphed from that crush-lust to something . . . more. Like I was thinking about dropping out of school and moving to Montana and living with his parents – who were like the sweetest people ever –'

'Wait. You were going to *move*?'

She shrugs. 'I was in love.'

'Who cares! You can't move! At least not until we go to college.'

'Oh, yeah,' she groans. 'College.'

'So, what happened?'

'It broke. The stupid condom *broke*. I mean, does that actually happen?'

'Apparently.'

'Yeah,' she says, 'apparently. We tried not to worry at first, but then I was late, and my parents found the pregnancy test because they were full-on going through my things at that point, and the shit just totally hit the fan. There were these *awful* meetings between our parents, and they would end up yelling and fighting and . . . Nate and I, we tried to stay out of it. Isn't that weird? We tried to stay out of these unbelievably major decisions about our life. And all the while I'm not allowed to tell anyone. Especially not you.'

'But why?'

'Because of the plan our genius parents came up with. My mom would raise Grace like she was her own baby, and Nate would spend his last year of high school at military school, and the two of us would never see each other again.'

'Oh my God, Pilar.'

She sniffs. 'I just didn't think it'd be that hard. But watching Grace call somebody else *Mommy*. It just . . . I couldn't do it.'

'So where's Nate now?'

Pilar looks at me and bursts out laughing. 'In our guest room.'

'Shut up!'

'I threw a total fit when my mom said she wasn't going to tell him what had happened to Gracie. He was working back on his parents' ranch, and caught a bus out here as soon as he heard.'

'Wow.'

'I know,' she says, blushing and laughing. 'My parents don't let us sleep in the same room, though.'

'So, what are you guys going to do?'

'I have no idea,' she says, sighing. 'Part of me thinks maybe I'll be with him forever, and then part of me is, like, wait, I'm sixteen, and how can the teenage brain even fully comprehend what "forever" means? So basically, I have no idea what I'm going to do.'

We fall silent again, Pilar's words and story echoing loudly in my head. I try to figure out how it makes me feel, if having the puzzle pieces is enough to make something whole again.

'So that's the story,' Pilar says.

'Some story,' I answer. I can't think of anything else to say. I want to *feel* something, the same feelings of friendship that I'd always felt, but all I feel is confusion.

'I'm sorry I lied to you,' she says. 'But you lied to me, too.'

'I know.' Of course. The confusion makes sense. Pilar's not the only one who put up the wall.

We've finally come to the beach, and are greeted by a squealing four-legged, four-armed ball of flannel and leather.

'Do you mind?' I ask Pilar, just before MayBe and Thea tackle us. 'They really want to see you.'

Pilar smiles but can't answer anything except for 'Oooof' before we're a tangle of hats and scarves and giggles and tears.

'We miss you!' MayBe finally says, working her way into Pilar's lap.

'Yeah, and Dylan won't stop mooning over your chair at lunch!' Thea says, flopping back in the snow. 'She's, like, useless without you.'

Pilar and I glance at each other. For a moment the wall is gone.

We pull one another upright, and then there are hugs and some tears, and then we realise we're freezing and in dire need of hot chocolate.

'My mom called just before you guys got here,' Thea says. 'She's in the parking lot. We can go to my house, if you want.'

Our walk back up the trail goes quickly. I walk next to Thea, behind MayBe and Pilar, listening to MayBe list the organic baby products she's been making and storing in her kitchen for Grace.

'How'd it go?' Thea whispers.

I shrug and swallow back the lump in my throat.

'It'll get better,' she says, nudging me. 'You guys just have to be OK hating each other a little bit. It makes it easier for the love to come back that way.'

We sit around Thea's table, her mom nervously piling cartons of cookies and ice cream in front of us until Thea says, 'Ma, please . . .' and her mom leaves.

Left in the quiet, familiar kitchen, MayBe and Thea keep looking at Pilar, and then at me.

'Fine,' Pilar says, turning to me. 'How are you?'

'Oh, you know,' I say, laughing nervously and stealing a glance to gauge her reaction. 'Psychic.'

She smirks. 'How's that going for you?'

'She set my socks on fire just by looking at them,' Thea says. 'Just kidding. Dylan, go ahead. Tell her about being psychic.' Thea hands me a cookie, like it will help me along. She looks at Pilar. 'She barely tells us anything. She wanted you to know first. Ask her if she can set things on fire just by looking at them. That's what I want to know.'

Pilar's laugh is thin, but it's there. She looks at me. 'Can you set things on fire just by looking at them?'

'No.'

Thea jumps in. 'Can you make cats bark and make it rain tampons?'

'No.'

'I told you,' MayBe says to Thea. I don't join their giggles. I just watch Pilar watch me, her face drawn.

'So what *can* you do?' she asks.

'I can see dead kids,' I answer. The giggling stops. I take a breath. 'I can see kids that have been taken. Sometimes they're alive, but most of the time they're dead.'

I've said that same thing a lot of times since what happened with Cate. I said it to my mom, and I said it on the phone to my aunts Ruby and Peg, who told me I needed to come visit this summer and *be theirs for a while*. I even said it to my grandma, who still refused to talk to my mom. I said it to myself, in the dark of my bedroom before I slept. I told my secret all those times, but none of them felt real, not until now, when I am saying out loud what I haven't even said to myself.

'I could have saved Clarence.'

Thea and MayBe moan in protest, reaching for me. I pull away, still looking at Pilar.

'I could have saved all of them, but I didn't. I was too afraid to know what I could do.'

'You were a kid,' Pilar says. 'You *are* a kid. It's not your fault, what you didn't know.'

'What if – if I didn't –' I stammer. 'What if Gracie . . .'

Pilar grabs my hand. Hers is ice cold. 'But you did. You did see her, Dylan. You weren't strong enough before, but you are now. You saved her. You saved my Gracie.'

'Oh my God, please just hug already!' Thea says, pushing me toward Pilar. We fall awkwardly into each other's arms. Pilar's grip on me is sudden and surprising, and it takes me a second to wrap my arms around her, to hold her against me, and to cry.

I'm not afraid of seeing things any more. I know that I won't be seeing them alone.

EGMONT PRESS: ETHICAL PUBLISHING

Egmont Press is about turning writers into successful authors and children into passionate readers – producing books that enrich and entertain. As a responsible children's publisher, we go even further, considering the world in which our consumers are growing up.

Safety First
Naturally, all of our books meet legal safety requirements. But we go further than this; every book with play value is tested to the highest standards – if it fails, it's back to the drawing-board.

Made Fairly
We are working to ensure that the workers involved in our supply chain – the people that make our books – are treated with fairness and respect.

Responsible Forestry
We are committed to ensuring all our papers come from environmentally and socially responsible forest sources.

For more information, please visit our website at
www.egmont.co.uk/ethicalpublishing

The Forest Stewardship Council (FSC) is an international, non-governmental organisation dedicated to promoting responsible management of the world's forests. FSC operates a system of forest certification and product labelling that allows consumers to identify wood and wood-based products from well-managed forests.

For more information about the FSC, please visit their website at www.fsc-uk.org